KID NORMAL
AND THE
SHADOW MACHINE

KID NORMAL
AND THE
SHADOW
MACHINE

GREG & CHRIS
JAMES SMITH

ILLUSTRATED BY
ERICA SALCEDO

BLOOMSBURY
CHILDREN'S BOOKS
NEW YORK LONDON OXFORD NEW DELHI SYDNEY

BLOOMSBURY CHILDREN'S BOOKS
Bloomsbury Publishing Inc., part of Bloomsbury Publishing Plc
1385 Broadway, New York, NY 10018

BLOOMSBURY, BLOOMSBURY CHILDREN'S BOOKS, and the Diana logo
are trademarks of Bloomsbury Publishing Plc

First published in Great Britain in March 2019 by Bloomsbury Publishing Plc
Published in the United States of America in October 2020
by Bloomsbury Children's Books

Bloomsbury books may be purchased for business or promotional use.
For information on bulk purchases please contact Macmillan Corporate and Premium
Sales Department at specialmarkets@macmillan.com

Library of Congress Cataloging-in-Publication Data
Names: James, Greg (Radio personality), author. | Smith, Chris
(Radio personality), author. | Salcedo, Erica, illustrator.
Title: Kid Normal and the shadow machine / by Greg James and Chris Smith ;
illustrated by Erica Salcedo.
Description: New York : Bloomsbury Children's Books, 2020.
Summary: Murph Cooper and the Super Zeroes get past some problems to capture
the planet's most dangerous supervillains after a jailbreak, but Magpie gets away and
teams up with another old enemy.
Identifiers: LCCN 2020016552 (print) • LCCN 2020016553 (e-book)
ISBN 978-1-5476-0331-2 (hardcover) • ISBN 978-1-5476-0332-9 (e-book)
Subjects: CYAC: Superheroes—Fiction. | Supervillains—Fiction. | Ability—Fiction. |
Schools—Fiction. | Humorous stories.
Classification: LCC PZ7.1.J38487 Kn 2020 (print) | LCC PZ7.1.J38487 (e-book) | DDC [Fic]—dc23
LC record available at https://lccn.loc.gov/2020016552

Printed and bound in the U.S.A. by Berryville Graphics Inc., Berryville, Virginia
2 4 6 8 10 9 7 5 3 1

All papers used by Bloomsbury Publishing Plc are natural, recyclable products made
from wood grown in well-managed forests. The manufacturing processes conform
to the environmental regulations of the country of origin.

To find out more about our authors and books visit www.bloomsbury.com
and sign up for our newsletters.

This one is for Jenny x

—Chris

*For Bella—who has been upgraded
to wife status since the last book.
You're the best thing ever x*

—Greg

1

The Mystery at the Standing Stones

What goes through the mind of a superhero in the moments before a battle? Thoughts of bravery? Dreams of triumph? A dash of fear? A thrill of excitement?

Mary Perkins was thinking about pies. She gripped the handle of her umbrella tightly and squinted out of the *Banshee*'s windshield at the watercolor crimson streaks of a late-October dawn painted across the sky ahead, as the Super Zeroes' car toiled and bumped along a very uneven forest trail. Her stomach was churning and sloshing like a washing machine full of soup.

The summons from the Heroes' Alliance had woken Mary in the small hours of the morning—her wristwatch-shaped HALO communication unit buzzing and flashing like an electric wasp trapped beneath the covers. But it wasn't just the rocky ride that was making Mary feel so sick, or the time of day. Mary was anxious and queasy for a whole host of other reasons too, none of which we can tell you about right now, because it would completely ruin the plot.

Nellie sat at the controls, silent as always, peering ahead through the trees with both hands gripping the control wheel of the silvery-blue car. The *Banshee* was equipped with twin jet engines, and the group could easily be roaring through the sky toward their destination. But the instructions from the Alliance had been clear: No flying. Approach as stealthily as possible. This was war—and the first rule of war is: always try to take the enemy by surprise.

Mary was sitting beside Nellie in the copilot's chair. She tried desperately to focus on the mission at hand, even though her brain was still filling itself with thoughts about pies. She glanced down at the screen in the center of the control panel.

"We should be almost there," she said without turning her head, twitching her glasses up her nose with one hand and tapping buttons with the other.

"Looks like there are several other Alliance units meeting us at the edge of the forest."

Behind her she heard a faint hissing noise and turned to see that one of Billy's ears had inflated. "Bit nervous," he whispered.

"We're all nervous, Billy," Mary replied. "We can't afford to mess this up . . ." A fresh wave of anxiety hit her, and her stomach performed a spectacular double somersault complete with a twist. "Again."

Billy grimaced, smoothing down his errant ear.

Mary could see Hilda behind him. She was sitting cross-legged on the cold metal floor at the back of the *Banshee*, gazing out at the forest as it rolled past. Even the normally bubbly red-haired summoner of tiny horses seemed tense. And Mary knew why.

With that thought, her gaze flicked to Murph Cooper. The leader of the Super Zeroes was sitting next to Billy. He was pale, quiet, and pensive. He was showing no interest in the control screen or, apparently, the upcoming mission. It was as if an invisible storm cloud of misery was radiating from him, raining drops of sadness across the whole team. He'd been like this for weeks now, and it was becoming impossible to ignore the impact it was having.

The reason Mary had been thinking about pies was this: she'd always imagined their little band of Heroes as a kind of pie. She, Billy, Hilda, and Nellie were like the filling. Individually they were all great ingredients, like meat, potatoes, vegetables, and gravy, but it was Murph who brought them together so successfully. His leadership was the crust that held the Super Zeroes in place. But over the past month, cracks had started to appear in that crust. Their pie was falling apart. And it was all because of a new, unwanted ingredient . . .

Mary watched Angel's silvery-blond hair reflecting light from the early-morning sun. She was sitting on the floor near Hilda, looking bright and enthusiastic as usual. Apparently Murph's drizzle of angst wasn't hitting her.

It's not that there's anything bad about Angel, Mary thought to herself. *It's just that she's the wrong ingredient for our pie. We're a delicious meat pie, and she's . . . well, she's . . .*

"She's jam," murmured Mary to herself decisively. That was it. *There's nothing wrong with jam in everyday life—it just has no place in a meat pie. In fact, it spoils the pie completely.*

"Did you just say, 'She's jam'?" asked Billy from behind her.

Mary sat up straight and blinked, once again tapping at the instrument panel. A small winged letter *Z* showed their own position. Several other symbols were converging on the same spot.

"I said, 'Jam . . . um . . . stand by,'" said Mary loudly. "We're here." Looking up and out of the windshield again, she could see that they were approaching the edge of the trees. A wide green field was visible beyond.

"Super Zeroes, halt at the tree line and stand by," crackled a voice over the radio.

"Roger and wilco," Nellie replied softly, reaching out her right hand to ease back on the throttle.

The *Banshee* slowed to a standstill at the very edge of the forest.

They were close to a huge clearing that sloped uphill to a jagged stone circle. Its monoliths were silhouetted against the crimson sky, and a deep

ditch had been dug near the crest of the low hill surrounding them.

"Oooooh, a henge!" exclaimed Hilda, moving up beside Mary. **"I love a good henge!"** The excitement of seeing an ancient monument seemed, for a second, to have overtaken her worries about the risk of another failed mission.

The rising sun was framed perfectly between two of the gigantic stones. Sunbeams fired across the clearing toward them, cutting through the misty dawn like lasers. It really did look extremely cool.

"All units in position" came a serious voice over the speaker. Mary glanced back down at the control panel. The symbols representing different Heroes' Alliance combat units were now arranged in a rough circle around the edge of the clearing. Whoever their target was, they had them surrounded.

"Attention all units" came the voice again. "This is your mission commander, Vapor Trail."

"Oh wow," said Hilda, wide-eyed. "Vapor Trail's, like, the best skimmer in the whole Alliance. **She's a total legend."**

Mary was heartened slightly by this news. Even if Murph wasn't going to shake himself out of his grump, at least the mission as a whole was in the hands of a highly skilled Hero.

"We have surrounded one of the key players in the Alliance of Evil," Vapor Trail went on. "He is known as The Druid. We have intelligence that he's on the verge of a major attack that could compromise us severely. His base is located underneath this stone circle."

"Henge," corrected Hilda quietly.

"Our mission for this morning is perfectly simple, people," went on their commander. "We will advance on the circle . . ."

"Henge," whispered Hilda.

"Shush!" Murph shushed her irritably. It was the first time he'd spoken in an hour.

". . . and contain The Druid and any other Rogues we might find there," continued the voice from the radio. "All wings report in."

"Super Zeroes responding," said Nellie into her silver headset. "Rain Shadow active . . ."

"Equana active," chimed in Hilda.

"Mary Canary active."

"Balloon Boy active."

"Kid Normal active," came Murph's flat, small-sounding voice.

"Angel active," completed Angel, filling Mary's brain with further thoughts of a jam-spoiled meat pie.

More voices were now checking in over the radio. Hilda's eyes regained some of their sparkle as she heard the names: "Ram-Man responding . . . Kid Convection responding . . . Lady Rhythm responding . . ."

"What do you think Lady Rhythm's Cape is?" Hilda said. "Do you think she says, 'The Rhythm is gonna get ya'?" She clicked her fingers on either side of her face and wiggled her head, attempting some amateur sass of her own.

Mary watched her friend fondly. Maybe this mission would be okay after all. In any case, it was their last chance.

"T-Rex responding . . . Dough-Boy responding . . . John responding . . ." the list over the radio continued.

"What sort of a Hero calls himself John?" Billy wondered. "There are a lot of Heroes here, you know.

This Druid character must be dangerous." His ear puffed up again at the thought.

"All units advance," Vapor Trail told the assembled Heroes. "On my signal, halt your vehicles and engage. Let's make sure The Druid doesn't get the chance to put his plan into action, and we'll be home in time for eggs and bacon."

Nellie moved the throttle gently forward. The *Banshee* rumbled out of the trees and started up the shallow gradient toward the standing stones.

Mary watched as more vehicles emerged into the chilly dawn light. To their left was a black-clad figure astride a large four-wheeler. On their other flank was a military-grade armored car, painted in a camouflage pattern. Beyond that was a group of five figures on motorcycles.

The Heroes converged on the stone circle. As they neared the wide, shallow ditch, Vapor Trail gave the signal.

"We've got him surrounded," barked her voice over the radio static. "Out of your vehicles and engage. Don't let him through the cordon! **Move, move, move!"**

Inside the *Banshee*, the Super Zeroes were all looking at Murph, waiting for him to leap into action. But he seemed lost in thought. Mary was about to speak up herself, when Angel took the initiative.

"Come on, then!" Angel urged the others, pushing herself to her feet and smacking the button that opened the side door. "You heard the woman—it's Hero time!"

The Super Zeroes followed Angel as she pelted down the ramp, gasping as the chilly early-morning air hit their tired faces. They took up position in front of the car, just where the ground sloped downward into the ditch.

"There he is!" shouted a voice away to one side.

In the center of the standing stones they could see a figure struggling out from a gap between two fallen boulders. It was a tall, thin man with a straggly beard. He was dressed in a long, pale-colored robe and sandals, and his long, unwashed hair trailed over his face.

"He doesn't look so scary," said Mary out of the corner of her mouth to Murph. "We've obviously caught him

by surprise in the middle of his organic spelt oatmeal."
She'd hoped to lift Murph out of his lethargy with some
of their old banter, but he didn't respond. If anything
he looked even more pale and sick than before. Mary
sighed inwardly. This mission was vitally important—
and if Murph wasn't going to lead them, they would
just have to do without him. They would be a crustless
pie. A stew, in fact.

**"Hey-do the dilly-do, ding-dong
a-dill-o!"** cried The Druid in a high-pitched,
nasal voice, looking at the ring of fearsome Heroes

arranged around his stone circle. *Henge*—sorry, Hilda.

"I see I have some guests for breakfast, dill the dill-o.

Hey nonny, ninny-neigh, ting-tang a-spimp-o."

"O-*kaaay* . . ." Mary turned to the others. "I think we're dealing with a grade-A, certified, one-banana-short-of-a-monkey-brunch kind of villain here."

Angel nodded and moved across to stand beside her. Murph stepped sadly into the background.

"Ping-pong, a-pill-o," continued The Druid, spinning around and hopping from leg to leg like an exotically

dressed heron on a hot beach. "My guests look like they want to play, holl the derry-doll. **Ka-BLAMBA!**"

He gestured with a wizened hand at the armored car next to the *Banshee*. There was a huge crash as a large bush grew out of the ground beneath the vehicle within seconds, flipping it over backward. It rolled down the hill and slammed into the trees below.

"Ha! Flower power!" screamed The Druid. "You just got rhododendron'd!"

"Charge!" shouted the voice of Vapor Trail from the other side of the circle.

Then they saw her—a tall woman with highly muscled arms and legs, floating a couple of yards off the ground. They watched as she flipped herself horizontal and flew directly at The Druid, leaving a smoky haze behind her in the dewy air.

But before she reached him, The Druid spun rapidly around, moving his hands together in a complicated gesture. A web of vines sprang up between two of the standing stones, and Vapor Trail was trapped as she tried to fly through. She struggled vainly as the tendrils twined their way around her arms and legs.

"Seize him!" she shouted desperately. "He can't get away!"

"Let's roll," shouted Mary to the others, pelting across the wide grassy ditch and up the other side toward the stones. Angel's silvery-blond hair flew to one side of her in the chilly breeze; Hilda's red curls bobbed on the other.

Several teams of Heroes had already converged on The Druid's lair, and they struck with all their might. They hit him with the power of their combined Capes, one Hero shooting bolts of fire at him from her wrists, and another attempting to trap him between thick sheets of ice that he conjured from nowhere. But The Druid was ready for them. Out of the earth he summoned saplings that shattered the ice and allowed him to scramble up on top of one of the stones. Then he held back the other Heroes by creating clumps of mistletoe that quickly filled the ditch with springy shoots that were impossible to cut through.

"Mistletoe the dilly-o!" he taunted them in his thin—and, let's be frank here—really, really irritating voice. **"Wing, wong a-willow."**

Next, a circle of trees sprang up around him, completely concealing him behind their golden, drooping branches.

"This is like watching one of those backyard makeover shows on fast-forward," panted Billy. "I wonder if he's going to add a fountain?"

"We're about to add a kick-his-butt fountain," said Hilda grimly. It didn't make a huge amount of sense, but give her a break. It's actually not that easy to make up quips in the middle of a battle, whatever the movies say.

Hilda's face creased in concentration, and her two tiny horses popped into existence. "Go and keep an eye on the New Age weirdo," she told them, and they cantered off between the willow trunks.

"Horsies!" Mary heard the surprised voice of The Druid say from behind his curtain of leaves. "Where did you spring from, my fine-fetlocked fellows? The derry-o," he added as an afterthought.

Mary looked around her. The Druid had disappeared into the clump of willow trees at the other side of the stone circle. Billy was beside her, and as she turned she saw Nellie appear between two of the enormous stones, with Angel following behind.

No other Heroes seemed to have made it this far—the only other person Mary could see was Vapor Trail, still struggling in her prison of vines.

"You four!" the commander shouted to them desperately. "Do something!"

"Where's Murph?" said Angel as she joined the others. "I thought he was behind me!"

Wide eyes and shaken heads were the only answer.

"He must have got caught in mistletoe-geddon back there, like everyone else," Mary hedged.

One of Hilda's horses was trotting back out from the impromptu willow thicket, tossing its mane. "Looks like he's still in there," interpreted Hilda.

"Nellie, time to charge yourself up," Mary instructed.

"Yeah, great idea!" enthused Hilda. "I just checked my watch, and it's Druid-electrocuting o'clock!" Again, let's cut her some slack here. It was a very tense moment.

Nellie concentrated, holding out one hand, palm upward. The clouds above them began to boil and thicken, and there was a sudden clap of thunder.

"Stormy-borm a-bill-bob!" they heard The Druid mutter to himself like a total loon.

Nellie set her face in a serious scowl and stalked toward the trees, one palm raised. A fork of slim silver lightning—so thin it looked like a delicate shard of cut glass—suddenly sparked between the dark clouds and her outstretched hand. Her palm began to glow with bolts of blue electricity.

Mary beckoned the others and followed.

"Go get him!" Billy encouraged Nellie in a whisper. "I'm right behind you if you need anything, um, you know . . . ballooning."

It was dark between the willows, and Mary had to squint through the gloom to make out the stone atop which The Druid had been squatting. He was nowhere to be seen—but suddenly she noticed one of the tiny white horses not far away from her, gesturing urgently with an upraised fore-hoof to one of the nearby trunks.

Nellie had seen it too.

Silently nodding her thanks, she pointed at the

tree. A bolt of lightning shot from her finger, slamming into the trunk and prompting a startled cry of **"Ow, get off! That hurt!"**

He's forgotten all about the ding-dong a-dill-o's now that the chips are down, thought Mary grimly to herself as Nellie fired another bolt.

The Druid leaped out from his hiding place, holding a hand to his singed posterior, which was emitting a very pleasing wisp of smoke. Like an overdressed squirrel, he grabbed a branch and swung himself into the boughs of the smoking tree, evading Nellie's lightning bolts as he scrambled rapidly upward.

"I'm out of charge," Nellie said to Mary, holding out her hand sadly. The blue electricity had indeed vanished.

"Back to the edge of the thicket," Mary ordered.

They were so close to capturing this Rogue. Hope flared inside her like a match striking. If they could go back to the Alliance in triumph, just this once . . . maybe everything would be forgiven.

Suddenly, at the edge of the willows, she saw the unmistakable flash of unwashed burlap between the leaves. This was her chance.

"There he goes!" she cried, drawing her umbrella out of her raincoat pocket like a medieval knight flourishing his sword. As she did so, she pressed the button so the handle extended and the yellow— canopy?—sprang open. We're not sure what that part of an umbrella is called, but you know what we mean, right? Anyway, Mary sprang into the air to head off The Druid, who was bending a large branch downward.

The Druid grasped the end firmly, kicked off the trunk with his feet, and used the branch like a catapult to *sproing* himself skyward. Mary tried to counter him in midair, but she was met with a jet of hibiscus that hit her in the face and knocked her backward.

The Druid landed on all fours atop one of the other standing stones and began to leap around the circle from stone to stone, like a runaway tree frog in unsuitable footwear. He quickly reached the other side of the circle and dropped out of sight.

Mary managed a shaky landing, brushing blooms off her raincoat, and raced after the other Super Zeroes, who were already giving chase—urged on by Angel. **"Don't let him get away!"** roared Vapor Trail, struggling to move as the vines entangling her started to wither away and vanish. The willow trees, too, had begun to wave themselves back into the ground like a garden makeover TV show in reverse.

As Mary dashed between two of the standing stones, she could make out The Druid crossing the wide ditch. He darted sideways, through the gap next to the *Banshee* where the armored car had been, and raced away down the hill.

"Back to the vehicles! After him!" came Vapor Trail's voice from behind her.

Mary broke into a sprint to try to catch up with Nellie, who was already pounding up the ramp into the *Banshee*. She arrived just in time to see their pilot throw herself into her chair, flicking switches as she did so and reaching for the throttle. But there was no sound—and no lights winking on the instrument panel. Nellie tapped the screen, looking bemused. It was blank.

"It won't start!" came a cry from outside. The Hero with the four-wheeler was kicking at the foot pedal in vain.

Mary turned and looked around at the other vehicles ranged around the brow of the hill. It quickly became apparent that not a single one of them would start. They could not give chase.

"Stand down, stand down!" Vapor Trail sounded furious as she strode across the ditch. "He's gone. Mission failed. Repeat, mission failed."

Mary walked slowly back down the ramp, exchanging worried glances with Billy and Hilda.

"Never mind." Angel tried to encourage them as she approached. "We did our best, didn't we? It's a shame Murph wasn't there to help, huh? What happened to . . . Oh, here he comes."

Mary turned to see Murph, disheveled and ashen-faced, climbing out of the ditch not far away. "Where were you?" she blurted out, only her icy shock keeping her temper in check.

"I got stuck . . . you know, in the, um, ivy . . . ?" muttered Murph, avoiding her eye.

Vapor Trail was scowling across at Mary as she spoke into her HALO unit: "Affirmative, he's escaped. Some Heroes did reach the target, but they were unable to capture him. **Mission failure.**"

Several hours later, the five Super Zeroes stood awkwardly on the rug in front of Miss Flint's large, polished wooden desk. Two burly Cleaners, dressed in their black uniforms, had been waiting for them as the *Banshee* landed. They had curtly dismissed Angel and brought the others here to face the head of the Heroes' Alliance.

Miss Flint's desk was littered with maps, letters, and important-looking documents, and a large screen up on the wall was flashing constant messages. ROGUE ACTIVITY REPORTED IN SECTOR 317A, read the urgent green letters. CLEANER INTERVENTION REQUIRED IN SECTOR 562T. She looked tired and stressed. And furious. Really, really furious.

"Well?" she snapped as soon as Mary had closed

the door behind them. "I'm told by Vapor Trail that you guys were in a prime position to stop The Druid from getting away, and you blew it. Another failed mission."

Out of the corner of her eye, Mary saw Murph step forward slightly. "It's not their fault," he began falteringly.

But Miss Flint looked in no mood to listen to explanations. At that moment a large red telephone on the desk began buzzing and flashing, and she snatched at the receiver. "Yes? Where? Dispatch any units you can spare. Now!" She slammed the phone down.

"Anything we can help with?" asked Mary meekly.

"You have got to be joking," replied Miss Flint scathingly. "On the basis of your recent missions, **I might as well send . . . I don't know. A cat!**" Miss Flint wasn't great at sarcasm, but her message was coming across loud and clear. "We're in the middle of a war here, in case none of you had noticed!"

There was an embarrassed silence. Nellie scuffed a toe of her sneaker across the swirly patterns in the rug.

Miss Flint sighed and clasped her hands in front of her. Her expression softened slightly as she looked around the room at the five of them, her gaze lingering on Murph in particular. "You all know that I have been your biggest champion," she said in a strained voice. "Especially since I've had to learn what it's like to be a Hero without a Capability. I had hoped that with Kid Normal at the helm, you would be a shining example of how the Heroes' Alliance could change for the better."

Mary felt a tiny warm nugget of hope. Maybe, just maybe, they were going to be given another chance to prove themselves.

"It seems I was wrong," continued Miss Flint.

The warm nugget of hope was plunged into a bucket of cold water, then placed on a flight to Antarctica with all the airplane windows open. And the in-flight meal was ice cubes.

The next three words Miss Flint said were, Mary decided, the three worst words in the entire universe, ever. Worse than "Kiss for Grandma", worse than "No Wi-Fi network", worse even than the previous record holders, "Pineapple on pizza".

"Hero status revoked," said the head of the Alliance, looking regretful but determined. "Please place your HALO units on the desk. You're being taken off active duty."

"What? No!" blurted out Hilda. **"But . . . there's a war going on!"**

"No buts," countered Miss Flint. "No 'What? No!'s. As you rightly point out, Miss Baker, there is a war on. And you are helping us lose it. You've become a danger to the Heroes' Alliance, and it can't be tolerated." She shuffled the papers on the desk back into order, seemingly unable to look the kids in the eye.

Mary felt mortified for herself, but even more so for poor Hilda, who had always been so proud of her status as a Hero. Surely, she thought, Murph wouldn't sit back and let this happen. Surely this would stir him to action. She looked across at him but was startled to see that he had already taken his HALO device off his wrist and was dropping it on Miss Flint's cluttered desk.

"Murph . . ." blurted out Mary. **"You're not . . . giving up?"**

Murph said nothing. She tried to read his expression as he pushed past her and out of the door, but he kept his head down. Shaking her head, Mary unfastened her own HALO unit, motioning for the other three to do the same. They dumped them beside Murph's, each making a dull clatter as it hit the wooden desk. Miss Flint's telephone rang again as they began to file out of the room.

"Yes, I can talk now," she snapped into the headset. "The issue's been dealt with." Her words were cut off as the heavy wooden door slammed closed behind them with soul-slapping finality.

Mary was even more aghast to see that Murph was already walking away from them. His slumped, defeated-looking back was some distance away, about to turn a corner in the long passageway.

"Hey!" she called after him furiously. Murph stopped, looking sheepish, as the four of them joined him.

Mary's mind was a jumble of frustration, confusion, and—she suddenly realized—anger. Perhaps Angel wasn't the reason their pie had failed. Maybe it was the limp, soggy crust that was supposed to hold everything together. After weeks of strain, Mary's kind and patient nature finally snapped, and she turned on their leader.

"Well, congratulations," she told him, her face burning. "You just got us kicked out of the Heroes' Alliance."

She was expecting Murph to snap back at her. A really good argument might have helped to clear the air. But instead, he just looked at her, ashen-faced and miserable.

He coughed slightly. "Look, I know I've let you down . . . ," he said softly.

"Let us down?" crowed Mary sarcastically. "Whatever makes you say that? Because we're basically trying to help the Heroes' Alliance fight this war without a leader? Because you just completely blew another mission by hiding in a ditch as The Druid scampered past you? Because you haven't been bothered about the Super Zeroes for ages, because you're too busy looking after Angel?" She felt tears of frustration bubbling at the corners of her eyes but was too furious to wipe them away.

"Easy, Mary," Billy broke in. "Murph would never blow a mission on purpose."

"And The Druid was a tricky customer," Hilda piped up. "I mean, the rest of the Alliance team didn't even get close to him. He managed to get one over on Vapor Trail and she's, you know, a real Hero."

"WE'RE supposed to be real Heroes!" raged Mary. **"We shouldn't be going all starry-eyed about the older crew!** Or be feeling inadequate because some of our Capes are a bit . . . well, weird. Or because our leader doesn't even have one." She felt her face flush. That had sounded more biting than she'd meant it to, but she was too frustrated to stop herself.

Murph looked truly stung at her mention of his lack of a Capability. "What happened to 'You don't need superpowers to be a hero'?" he asked quietly.

Mary stared him in the eye, shaking with anger. Some part of her brain was telling her to stop—that there were some things that you just couldn't take back once they'd been said. But it was too late. She heard the words coming out of her mouth with a kind of cold horror: "Well, maybe you do need them, Murph. Maybe you do."

We've all said things we don't mean when we've been angry or scared or frustrated. "I hate you." "We're not friends anymore." "Yes, the cauliflower sounds delicious, thanks, please give me an extra-large helping." As soon as the words are out, you wish you could reach out and grab them back. But words—and especially the wrong words—are one-way, unstoppable missiles. Launch them at your peril: you never know who's going to get hurt.

The silence roared in Mary's ears. She realized she'd gone too far, but she'd been desperate to say something—anything—that would get a reaction. She just wanted to see even a flash of the old Murph. The one who would talk back to her—bicker, disagree,

laugh at her sarcasm or raise his eyebrows in mock weariness.

But he said nothing.

Without a word, Murph turned sharply away and walked off down the corridor, leaving the remaining four Super Zeroes staring dumbstruck after their leader.

A few minutes later, Mary, Hilda, Billy, and Nellie were sitting in the *Banshee* preparing for takeoff. "I guess we'd better offer Carl the keys back," Mary said sadly, looking

around at the bare, functional cockpit with its familiar smell of oil and warm leather.

"Is Murph . . . coming with us?" asked Hilda in a small voice.

"I don't know," Mary replied flatly. "I just don't know what's going on with him, to be honest." She sighed. "I suppose I'd better go and see. Carry on with the preflight checks," she instructed Nellie, who nodded, head bent over her clipboard.

Mary returned to the spot where Murph had walked away from them. The passageway ended in a sturdy wooden door. After she opened it, she found herself in a large ornamental garden. Its tall shrubs and frozen fountains were coated with crystals of frost. Mary's breath condensed in the chilly early-evening air as she crunched down a pathway, following the footprints that were clearly marked in the gravel.

She could hear faint voices coming from up ahead of her. One of them was quiet and calm, but the other sounded angry.

The footprints left the path and wandered across a patch of frozen grass, so her own footsteps were muffled as she approached a large hedge, and peeped around the edge. Murph was sitting alone a little way away from her on a wooden bench. Mary spotted a glow in his hand and realized he was talking into one of the Heroes' Alliance's old HALO units, the ones that looked like phones. But who was he using it to talk to?

Mary strained her ears to hear through the misty, cold air.

"Did you succeed in your task today?" The voice was deep and mocking, and Mary had to clamp a hand to her mouth to stop herself from screaming in shock and horror as she heard it. She would have recognized that voice anywhere.

It belonged to the most feared supervillain in the world. A Rogue with the ability to steal superpowers. The greatest enemy of the Heroes' Alliance.

It was the voice of Magpie!

Mary felt winded by what Murph said next. "Yes," he replied. "I managed to sabotage the mission. I disabled the electronics in the vehicles with a TEMP unit."

"Splendid," gloated the voice. "Really, really splendid. My associate was able to escape, and I hear he has something rather special planned that will keep those fools in the Heroes' Alliance on their toes. Little suspecting that you are right in their midst . . ."

Mary felt as if the whole world had tilted and twisted around her. *Murph* had sabotaged their mission against The Druid! She felt as if she must be dreaming.

Was Murph . . . working with Magpie?

2

The Alliance of Evil

ONE MONTH EARLIER...

Wait . . . what?

Oh no, you didn't!

Yes, I'm afraid we went there. The most irritating trick in the whole authoring book. The old "one month earlier" ploy. Suckered you in with an exciting bit, and now we're going to fill in the backstory.

We realize that some of you might find this extremely annoying, and reader feedback is very important to us. So if you have any complaints about the use of the "one month earlier" plot device, please put them in writing and send them to:

Narrative Device Complaints Department
Third crater on the left
The Moon
Space

Thanks. And now let's get on with it, shall we? Then we can all be friends again.

ONE MONTH EARLIER...

"Murph! It's eight eighteen and thirty-four seconds!"

Who needs one of those smart speakers that tells you the time when you've got a parent? thought Murph to himself as he schlupped cheerfully down the stairs.

If you're not familiar with "schlupping" down the stairs, that's because it's a word we just made up. But if you want to give it a go, here's a beginner's guide. Schlupping 101, if you will. Schlupping can only be successfully accomplished in your socks. Feet together, you place your toes over the edge of each step, then tilt your feet forward until you slide onto the next stair down. You then use your toes as tiny caterpillars to inch yourself forward until you are in a position to schlupp once more. It's really very satisfying, and Murph was having an extremely rewarding Monday-morning schlupp, despite the increasingly urgent time bulletin updates rising to meet him with every stair.

His feet slid across the final step like a pair of synchronized snowboarders and bore him onward toward the kitchen.

"The whole area is still sealed off," the reporter on the radio was saying, *"with many local residents saying they saw multicolored flashing lights and several jets of fire shooting into the air during the night. The authorities are insisting this was simply a gas explosion. However, one eyewitness reports seeing what appeared to be a human figure actually flying toward the scene. Meanwhile . . ."*

Murph grinned as he poured himself a juice and began to ponder the cereals. Two weeks ago, there had been a mass jailbreak at Shivering Sands, the top-secret prison where the Heroes' Alliance held all the most dangerous Rogues. The Alliance had managed to recapture a small number of escapees, but many were still on the loose. It sounded to Murph like several Heroes had been in action overnight, rounding up one more.

Please let it be Magpie, Murph thought, even though he knew it was unlikely. Magpie was Shivering Sands' most dangerous inmate and he had masterminded the prison break. But despite the Alliance's best efforts to find him, he was still on the run. There'd been no sign of the villain since he fled his base inside a secret bunker after Murph and the Super Zeroes tracked him there.

At least we managed to rescue Angel, Murph reflected. Angel was the daughter of their friends Flora and Carl. She'd been trapped inside Magpie's base for thirty years, frozen in time, before they succeeded in freeing her. All in all, it had been a fairly eventful autumn.

"Busy day at school planned?" His mom broke into his thoughts, looking at him brightly from above her favorite coffee mug. Murph winced inwardly. Conversation at this hour was surely against some sort of law. He made a small **"prrrpt"** noise in reply, blowing bubbles into the milk on his poised spoon.

"What subjects have you got on a Monday morning?" she persisted.

Murph considered his answer. The honest reply would be, "Well, since I go to a school for kids with superpowers, normally we'd start with an hour of Capability Training, where all the other students except me learn to control

38

their abilities. But in fact today my best friends and I have been given the day off school because we're the youngest team of Heroes ever to join the Heroes' Alliance, and we've been called to a mysterious meeting at their top-secret headquarters." But given that his mom knew nothing about his double life, that wouldn't fly. Not even if he added the important detail "And we're traveling there in our own flying jet car." So instead, as always, he decided to gloss over most of the details with a complete lie.

"We've got geography, then double science," he answered.

"And you're doing all right, aren't you?" his mom asked, reaching over to pat his non-cereal hand. "Everything okay with your friends? **Nothing you want to talk about?** *Mary* **okay?"**

Murph shot her a glance. As expected, she had her friend-and-counselor-not-just-mom expression in place. "Yeahfinewhywouldyouevenaskabout Mary," he mumbled reluctantly.

The trouble was, no matter how brilliant his mom might be, Murph just couldn't open up to her. Tempting though it was to blurt out, **"I'M A SECRET**

SUPERHERO AND MY BEST FRIEND MARY CAN FLY," he knew it would go down badly. Disbelief would quickly be followed by the whole "Why has it taken you over a year to tell me this?" conversation. So instead he had to settle for acting like a typical twelve-year-old who was embarrassed about confiding in his mom.

"Smurphy-Bom-Burphy!" A hand ruffled his hair as his big brother, Andy, big-brothered his way into the kitchen and started fiddling with the toaster like he'd invented it. "Morning, Mom!"

Andy was eighteen and went to college across town, traveling there and back on the bus with his bag of books in a very grown-up fashion.

"How's secret school, then?" Andy asked nonchalantly, squiggling squeezy honey onto his toast from a height, like an overrated artist.

Andy was fascinated by Murph's school, and never tired of trying to ferret information out of him about it. He had a sibling's unerring sixth sense that there might be something there that could be used to tease, make fun, or otherwise torment.

"Pretty cool," Murph answered him evenly, chasing the last few runaway cereal flakes around the milk. "Nothing to report."

"No, there never is, is there?" mused Andy. "Very strange. When can I come and have a look around?"

"You can't," replied Murph, a little too quickly. He stood up and grabbed his backpack from the chair by the door, making ready for a smooth exit.

"What about Field Day? Can I come and watch?"

"Don't think they have one," answered Murph truthfully. In fact, all Field Days had been canceled until further notice after an incident with a stray Capability last year that had left two people in the hospital when the 200-meter sprint got over-competitive.

"What about Parents' Night?" asked Andy through a mouthful of toast, just as Murph was heading out of the door.

Murph stopped dead. **"P-P-Parents' Night?"**

"Ooh, yes!" chimed in their mom. "Parents' Night! Did I miss it last year?"

"Blurp . . . um . . . yerp, you must have," said Murph, his mind grinding away like an expiring tractor engine. "I think you were working."

"Ooh, well, when's the next one?"

"Next Thursday," lied Murph before he could stop himself.

"Why on earth did you just say 'Next Thursday,' you total idiot?" said the thinking part of his brain to the talking part.

"*I panicked!*" the talking part replied. "*Sorry!*"

"You're always sorry, and you never learn, do you?" the thinking part fumed. "*How many times do we have to go through this? All speech has to be run past me first, before you go flapping your mouth-parts like a hulking great head of lettuce!*"

Murph realized that while this internal brain-fight was going on, he was standing in the doorway with his mouth open, looking as if his batteries had suddenly run down.

"Yeah . . . next Thursday," he confirmed, twisting his face into a winning smile.

"Oh, I literally give up! He just

said it again," raged thinky-brain melodramatically.

"Great! I'll make sure I get the evening off," his mom told him. "Can't wait!"

"Okay . . . Well, huzzah!" burbled Murph. "Got to run now," he shouted over his shoulder as he left. "Don't want to be late for school . . ."

". . . *where you must now find the principal and tell him that he has to stage an entire fake Parents' Night,"* his brain silently completed as he galumphed down the front path. But Murph's mood wasn't dented. He was a member of the Heroes' Alliance, the head of a team of crime-fighting best friends. Nothing could possibly spoil that . . .

"The Heroes' Alliance is finished!" cried the man in the tattered black

coat, slamming his hand down onto the table, palm first. There was a rumble of approval from around the room.

The large chamber was packed with people. Well, we say "people" . . . It was certainly packed, and many of the figures gathered around the enormous central table could loosely be described as person-like. But they were an assorted bunch. Some enormous, some tiny. Some fat, some thin, some shaped like animals or monsters. For this was a gathering of Rogues, of villains. Of anyone whose aim was chaos, disorder, or crime.

Magpie had wasted no time in the two weeks since his escape from Shivering Sands. He had put the word out among the Rogues who he had allowed to escape, summoning them here, to his new lair. Promising them all that they would hear something to their advantage. And the message had spread across the hidden network of evil like poison through veins. From far and wide they had answered his call, hungry with the prospect of very, very bad things.

"It is time we rid the world of these so-called Heroes once and for all," Magpie continued, spitting the last word out scornfully like a bad sprout. He leaned back and smoothed his long hair with a long-fingered hand, looking around the table at the assembled crowd. This new plan was less than ideal.

He had hoped to have plenty of time alone in his secret bunker to plot his next move. But that was no longer possible . . . *All thanks to Kid Normal*, he thought to himself, his lip curling in scorn and hatred. His fingers fidgeted and tapped upon the tabletop with a restless rhythm.

"Along with many of you, my friends, I was held prisoner by those clowns."

"Hey!" complained a hugely loud voice. An enormous figure at the other end of the table leaned forward, its bulbous red nose catching the light. "'Clown' is not an insult!"

"I beg your pardon, my friend," soothed Magpie, controlling his irritation. He needed these fools, at least for a while. "I didn't mean to be . . . clownist. But I was about to tell you how we can take our revenge on the Heroes' Alliance."

"Now you're talking!" screamed the clown delightedly. "Time to give them a little party. And by 'party,'" he explained, looking around at the frankly astonishing collection of people gathered at the table, **"I mean KILL THEM! Aha, ha-ha, ha-haaaaa!"**

There was a smattering of applause in response to this, and a few whoops. It was the kind of speech villains really respond to: concise, easy to follow, and ending with the words "kill them."

Magpie frowned. He was in danger of losing the room.

"Yes!" he agreed quickly, getting to his feet to try to regain everyone's attention. "Indeed we will wreak a terrible revenge on the Heroes' Alliance!"

"Kill them!" shouted someone. There was another smattering of whoops.

"Yes, yes," soothed Magpie, flapping a hand, "kill them. Absolutely. But I was going to say a little more first—"

"Skip to the end!" shouted another voice. "The bit where you go, **'Kill them!'"**

There were cheers, and someone started a chant. **"Kill . . . them. Kill . . . them. Kill . . . them."**

Magpie had developed enormous patience during his time in prison, but this was the limit. He looked around for the person who had shouted, "Skip to the end"—it was a portly man in a black jumpsuit with white sleeves.

"Might I ask who you are, my friend?" asked Magpie smoothly.

"I . . . am Penguin Man!" cried the black-and-white-clad man, getting to his feet and displaying the fact that he did not have the perfect figure for such a tight-fitting jumpsuit. (Not that we're judging, you understand. This isn't some "worst-dressed supervillain" thing. We totally support the rights of everyone, maniacal villains included, to wear absolutely what they like. It's just that, with his tiny short legs, huge tummy, and thick, stumpy arms and a badge that says "I Heart Antarctica", the jumpsuit made him look really very much like . . . well, a penguin. Which, come to think of it, was the whole point of his outfit selection. So just ignore us. He nailed it.)

"Yes, Penguin Man!" he cried. "Due to a hideous accident in a DNA laboratory—which often seems to happen"—there was a rumble of agreement: many of the villains in the room were the product of accidents in DNA laboratories—"my DNA was fused with that of a penguin! So as well as the intelligence and speech of a man, I also have all the most evil attributes of . . . a penguin! A-ha ha ha ha!"

"And what are those?" asked a woman on his left, crossing her legs and looking at him skeptically.

"Well . . . I can survive extreme cold . . . by huddling together with other penguins," blustered Penguin Man. "And like the mighty penguin . . . I am completely flightless."

"That's not a power!" Somebody scoffed.

"Shut up!" squawked Penguin Man angrily, his pale, plump face flushing with anger. "I can swim as fast as the fastest-swimming species of penguin, the flamboyant gentoo penguin. Up to twenty-two miles an hour, and . . ."

Magpie decided that he had heard enough. He needed a show of strength to remind everyone who was in charge here, and he was pretty sure his evil plan could work just as well without the assistance of a crazed half man, half flightless-Antarctic-dwelling bird.

Just as Penguin Man was screeching, "I can incubate the eggs of the female penguin under a flap of skin", Magpie clicked his fingers and Penguin Man abruptly disappeared in a ball of flame with a startled **_"Kark!"_**

"Does anybody else feel like interrupting me?" asked Magpie quietly.

The assembled villains shook their heads, shuffling their chairs away from the spot where Penguin Man had been sitting. The room was filling with the smell of roasted bird, which was not unpleasant. Kind of like chicken.

"Excellent," said Magpie casually. "Now, where was I?"

"You were going to wreak a hideous vengeance upon the Heroes' Alliance," the clown prompted him in an uncharacteristically quiet-especially-for-a-giant-clown voice.

"Thank you, Party Animal," said Magpie. "Yes, I have asked you to gather here, my friends, because you have all been treated as freaks, as outcasts. The Heroes' Alliance, with its pathetic ideas about 'good' and 'virtue' has pursued you, persecuted you, imprisoned you. It is time to get our own back."

He raked the air with his long nose, looking back and forth around the table once more at the array of characters who had responded to his summons. His eye was caught by a lumpy, orange-colored creature with two large eyes set in the front of what was presumably its head. "You, for instance," said Magpie to the soft-looking mass, "you too were held in their inhumane prison—in Shivering Sands?"

The lumpy orange creature got to its feet, causing the villains on either side to gag.

"What on earth is that horrible smell?" said someone in a stage whisper.

"I am The Sponge," said the orangey-colored thing in a ponderous, bubbly voice. "I am entirely made out of bath sponge, so I can absorb any attack."

"It smells like wet dog around here!" coughed the Rogue next to him. The Sponge looked slightly embarrassed.

"I'm afraid I haven't dried quite properly," it admitted. "I may have a slight damp-sponge smell." It waved an arm apologetically, and there was a fresh bout of coughing and retching.

"Stop moving around!" someone said desperately.

"And you were held prisoner?" prompted Magpie, raising his eyebrows encouragingly.

"I was," confirmed The Sponge, squelching slightly

as it frowned. "The Heroes' Alliance didn't even put me on trial."

"You see!" screeched Magpie, looking around the table once again. He was slightly startled to see what appeared to be a large pig in a suit off to his left, but he controlled his surprise. "They lock us up! They are tyrants! They operate completely without mercy! It is time to rise up against them!" There was a general cheer at this. "They formed an alliance against us, because they consider us, according to their ridiculous, narrow worldview, 'evil.'" Magpie's wrinkled face twisted with scorn. "Well, if that's how they see us, that's how we shall attack them. I propose we form our own alliance! The Alliance of Evil!"

"Ooooh, that's very catchy," said the pig in a snuffly voice. Others agreed.

"If you join my Alliance of Evil," Magpie continued, raising his voice, "I will help you take your revenge on the world that has scorned you! I will allow you to bring all your most evil plans to fruition!"

"And how will you do that, dill the dilly-o?" asked

a tall man with a straggly beard. He was sitting back on his chair with his sandaled feet on the table.

"I was hoping you'd ask," replied Magpie, barely even thrown by this display of unacceptable footwear manners. "DoomWeasel, reveal our spoils!"

A small man who had been squatting on the floor behind Magpie stroking a rather cute rat got to his feet, unleashing a blast of trash smell that made the northern-most half of the assembled villains gag. It wafted across the room, meeting the stench of partially dried sponge and the waft of flash-fried penguin coming from the other direction and creating a perfect storm of odors about halfway down the table. Even the large pig, no stranger himself to strong odors, retched slightly.

DoomWeasel capered to the back of the room like a partially decomposed jester, shedding bits of eggshell and a trail of greeny-brown footprints behind him. He pressed a few buttons on a control panel beside a pair of large metal doors, and they lumbered open. The room fell entirely silent.

Behind the doors was a room filled to the ceiling with enormous amounts of money. Thick wads of bills

were haphazardly piled in heaps, and gleaming bars of gold were stacked up like the world's most expensive game of Jenga. Every single Rogue stared in wonder at the sight, dumbstruck, their mouths open like a school of greedy fish (one of whom is pig-shaped).

Magpie didn't even turn around. He had known the effect this would have, and he stood drinking in the expressions of naked greed arranged around him. These idiots would do anything he wanted.

"As I was saying . . ." He spoke quietly, aware that

every single ear in the room was fixated on him. "I can enable you to bring all your most evil plans to fruition. You, for instance"—he pointed to a green-clad woman a few seats away—"what is your plan?"

"I am Ground Force!" she shrieked, shaking out her crinkly red hair with a wicked laugh. "And I plan to take over the world . . . one garden at a time!"

Magpie wished inwardly that he'd picked a better person to start with, but he inclined his head patronizingly and said, "Well, my green-fingered friend, I can help you buy as much . . . um . . . gardening equipment as you desire to make that happen."

"And I," said a smartly dressed woman sitting nearby, "I am The Architect! I want to tear down attractive old buildings and replace them with slightly disappointing modern equivalents!"

There was a cheer from around the room. The rest of the newly formed Alliance of Evil clearly thought this was an especially dastardly plot.

"And what is your power? Can you shoot concrete out of your wrists?" asked Magpie.

"Um, no, I don't actually have a power," the woman replied. "I am, quite literally, an architect. But quite an evil one." The room cheered again anyway.

"I want to start up my little Carnival of Chaos once more!" boomed Party Animal, producing a balloon from nowhere, which exploded dramatically, adding a smell of scorched rubber to the smorgasbord of stinks already present.

"Well, I'll be happy to finance your carnival," said Magpie. "In fact, I am proposing to supply all of you with any funds you require to put your evil schemes into action. There is only one condition . . ." Everyone looked at him suspiciously. Villains hate a catch. "You must waste no time in planning your attacks! They should begin at once! With the combined might of us all against them, the Heroes' Alliance will be overwhelmed within days!" Everyone sighed with relief. This was a catch they could get on board with.

"Do we have a deal?" roared Magpie.

"Yes!" said everyone, although it was badly coordinated, so it kind of sounded more like

"Yrrraaaarrrgggs!!" But it was unmistakably a noise of agreement.

"Then welcome, my friends, to the Alliance of Evil!"

"Wrooooarrrrgh!"

"We shall confound, confront, and defeat those goody-goody nobodies!"

"Breeeerrrreeeeersch!"

Magpie began to circulate around the table, shaking hands with his new allies. When he got to the pig, he unthinkingly held out a hand. The pig, looking confused, held out a trotter. Magpie looked down. The room fell silent again. This was a social minefield nobody had ever encountered before.

Finally, after what seemed like about eight seconds but was in fact only seven, Magpie clenched his spindly fingers into a fist and extended his hand in what can only be described as a trotter bump. The pig grinned an evil grin and Magpie tossed his long hair in relief. **"Down with Heroes!"** he screeched.

"Down with Heroes!" answered the assembled villains, taking up the chant. "Down with Heroes! Down with Heroes! Down with Heroes!" they thundered as Magpie, smiling cruelly to himself, turned on his heel and slipped out through a side door.

"Down with Heroes! Down with Heroes! Down with Heroes!" chirped DoomWeasel as he followed his master through the doorway and up a metal staircase.

"Silence!" snapped Magpie, turning through a door and along a metal passageway lined with old, rusting panels of dials and switches.

He rubbed his eyes as he walked. Magpie had always preferred to work alone, and thirty years in prison had made him even more solitary. Having to deal with so many other people on a daily basis, especially people like DoomWeasel, whom he found deeply pathetic, was exhausting. It was all he could do not to unleash the myriad of Capabilities swirling around within him and blow the little man to smithereens. But he kept himself in check. For now, he needed to use these insects. And then, when he had his final victory over Kid Normal . . . then he could finally be alone. Magpie smiled to himself and turned to DoomWeasel.

"I have a job for you, my friend," he said evenly, plastering an unconvincing smile across his lined, pinched face. At least he could get rid of this ridiculous creature for a while.

"Name it! DoomWeasel will do anything to smash the Heroes' Alliance!" squeaked the little man as he scampered along in Magpie's wake. "Along with my dastardly sidekick, the great Ratsputin!" The small brown face of DoomWeasel's pet rodent peeped out of one of his pockets and uttered a tiny and not-at-all evil-sounding **"scree!"**

"Yes, my friend," soothed DoomWeasel, "soon all Heroes shall learn to fear you!"

"Meep," agreed the rat as the little man capered around, cackling with delight.

Magpie controlled his temper, once again with some difficulty. "Soon, yes," he told DoomWeasel. "But first I want you to go and seek out more evildoers to join our cause, my faithful sidekick."

Magpie had meant this to be ingratiating, but the other man bridled.

"DoomWeasel is not a sidekick!" he squeaked. **"I am the main kick!"**

"Do as I tell you!" snapped Magpie, fury flashing in his eyes. For a moment there was a thickening in the air—an electrical prickle like an oncoming storm.

DoomWeasel cowered, although if Magpie had looked more closely at his face, he would have seen an expression of hidden spite, like a whipped dog longing to bare its teeth.

"I shall do as you ask . . ." DoomWeasel replied sullenly.

"Master!" insisted Magpie, running out of patience.

"Master," repeated DoomWeasel, with another tiny, unseen, undared flash of defiance in his eyes.

After giving the little man his instructions, Magpie dismissed him and stood for a moment in silent thought. Then his long, pale fingers closed on a door handle, and he stepped into a side room.

In stark contrast to the rest of the building, this space was warm and comfortable. A cheerful fire burned in the grate, and an armchair stood before it. From the doorway Magpie could see a pair of legs stretched out toward the flames, the flickering light bouncing back from the extremely shiny shoes on the ends of them.

"Good evening" came a voice from the chair. **"Was your meeting satisfactory?"**

"Very much so," answered Magpie. "Later today I shall deliver my declaration of war to the Heroes' Alliance. And then . . ."

The man in the chair stood and turned around to face him. He had carefully oiled hair and a long, sharp nose. His manicured appearance and immaculately pressed suit were a million miles away from Magpie's straggly black-and-white hair and ragged coat, and yet if you were to see them side by side you would

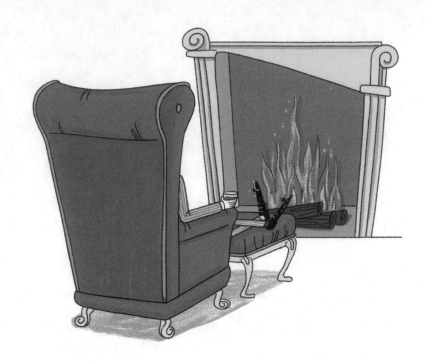

notice a similar expression in the eyes of both men.

A hunger for power. An ambition. A lack of regard

for consequences.

"And then we can begin our real work," completed Nicholas

Knox with a slow, chilling smile.

3

Witchberry Hall

It was one of those blazing October days when summer knows it's staying up too late but is having far too much fun to go to bed just yet. The scattering of small puffy clouds in the sky were just there for decoration. It was, Murph thought to himself, the perfect day not to be going to school. He looked across at Nellie in the pilot's chair of the *Banshee*. His friend's face was set with concentration as she carefully followed the line of the canal that wandered through the countryside below them, gradually easing forward on the control stick to bring the flying car lower. Squinting against the sun, she steered them to the left above a patch of woodland and dropped lower still, until they were skimming along at rooftop height along an avenue of trees.

"There it is!" said Murph, pointing.

"The new headquarters of the Heroes' Alliance!" breathed Hilda excitedly.

Ahead of them, at the end of the double row of tall oaks, stood a large, red-brick mansion. Its stone steps led up to imposing double doors and a simply unnecessary number of windows—in fact, it had everything you usually get in a house of that size except for a gift shop and café. Along the front was a row of much smaller trees, covered with thick clusters of bright red berries.

"Come in, *Banshee*, this is Witchberry Control," crackled a familiar voice over the radio.

"It's Jasper!" exclaimed Hilda.

"Well, this is his house, after all," reasoned Murph.

"*Banshee* receiving, may you give us permission to land, please?" said Nellie softly into her headset.

"Roger that, *Banshee*, you can set down in the kitchen garden on the south side," answered the voice of Sir Jasper Rowntree. "But watch out for the herbs!"

Nellie pulled back on a control lever and the car slowed. There was a scream from the twin jet engines as it hovered above the grass.

Attached to one side of the hall was a large walled garden with small blinking lights at each corner. Nellie piloted the car above this and set it down as gently as she could inside the crumbling brickwork. As she did so, a wooden door in the side of the house opened, and a neatly dressed elderly man zoomed out into the garden in a high-tech electric wheelchair. His silk scarf tugged and flapped in the rush of wind from the *Banshee*'s jets. Murph watched him waving his arms and apparently shouting something as he wheeled over toward a long flower bed that was bright with green foliage.

The noise of the jets died away, and Nellie pushed the button to open the main door, flicking switches confidently with her other hand as she did so. With a whine, the door at the side of the car slid open and a ramp extended.

"Watch the herbs, I said!" Sir Jasper was shouting. **"You're perturbing my lemon balm, you young hooligans!"** But the smile on the old man's face told Murph his friend was joking.

"Kid Normal!" Jasper cried in greeting as Murph walked down the ramp. "Greetings and salutations, young fella. And welcome to Alliance headquarters. **Welcome to Witchberry Hall!"**

"Thanks," replied Murph, receiving a firm handshake. "Um, nice house."

"Yes, not too bad, is it?" Sir Jasper mused. "Heating bills are a total nightmare though. Now, where are the rest of your motley crew, *mein Kapitän*? Ah, here they come. Lady Horsey-Horse. Summoner of miniature stallions!"

"It's Equana, actually," said Hilda, smiling despite herself as she stepped out of the *Banshee*. "Hello, Jasper."

"Puffing Billy! With the miraculous ability to inflate body parts—usually by accident!"

"Balloon Boy." Billy grinned. "Hiya."

"Mary, Mary, extremely contrary," teased Jasper as Mary emerged. "Our daffodil-hued flying Hero."

"How extremely dare you!" she mock-scolded him, smoothing her yellow raincoat. "That's Mary Canary to you."

"And where's the pilot? Our weather-controller? Where's Rain Shadow?" queried the old man.

"Hey, how come only Nellie gets her proper Hero name?" complained Billy.

Back in the cockpit, Nellie removed her slim silver headset and hung it carefully beside her. She grabbed a clipboard from the control panel and checked off a couple of readouts.

"Old Carl's trained you well, I see." Sir Jasper congratulated her, rolling up the ramp. "Post-flight checks all in order?"

Nellie nodded, shaking her hair over her face. She was still slightly uncomfortable speaking out loud, unless she was in midair in control of the *Banshee*, when all her shyness seemed to vanish. The *Banshee*'s original owners—Flora and Carl—had given the Super Zeroes the miraculous car after they had rescued Angel, and since then Murph had suggested on more than one occasion that Nellie should wear her pilot's headset at all times.

"Come on then," encouraged Sir Jasper. "Let's get inside. I want to show you around my workshop before the meeting starts. Got a surprise for you!"

Inside, the huge house was all bustle. Almost immediately, they had to press themselves against the wall of a long, stone-floored passageway as a squad of serious-faced women and men in black military uniforms marched past. They were Cleaners—the highly efficient and more-than-a-bit-mysterious soldiers of the Heroes' Alliance tasked with keeping its activities secret from the general population.

"We've had to set everything up here pretty darned sharpish," chattered Sir Jasper to them as they continued down the corridor. "When Magpie hacked into the HALO system during the prison break, he got access to a lot of the Alliance's secrets. Locations, personnel, equipment . . . We don't know how much he learned before we shut the whole system down, but for safety's sake we've had to move things underground. Luckily, a lot of the right technology was here already, back from when Carl and I used to do all our inventing and tinkering here as youngsters. Open!"

They had arrived outside a large metal door with the word **Workshop** stenciled on it in big black letters. At Sir Jasper's command a panel set into the wall beside it flashed green, and a metallic voice intoned, **"Voice print authenticated. Access granted."** The door slid open smoothly, and everyone gasped.

The workshop was a cavernous room, dug deep into the ground below Witchberry Hall. The only natural light came from rows of large windows right along the top of each high wall. The door they had just walked through was at the top of a wide set of stairs, so Murph had an overview of the whole space. He could see rows of benches, each one lighting up periodically with sparks and jets of flame as technicians busily assembled equipment. Several half-built vehicles were arranged along the opposite wall—cars, motorcycles, and even a partially assembled speedboat with a gleaming varnished wooden deck.

At one end of this row was a matte-black car with twin helicopter blades. It was hanging below a large pair of closed metal doors that were set into the ceiling. Murph immediately recognized it as Sir Jasper's own personal transport, Gertie.

Nellie couldn't stop herself from rushing forward with her mouth open. She looked as excited as a chicken who's just learned that the value of eggs has skyrocketed.

"This . . . is the coolest place ever, ever!" she breathed to herself as she galumphed her dirty white sneakers down the stairs.

She walked straight up to the nearest bench, where a women in large plastic safety glasses was screwing a flashing control panel onto a silvery bulletproof vest. The woman smiled and beckoned Nellie closer. Murph could see her point out the details of the circuitry she was working on.

"It's been nonstop, as you can imagine," Sir Jasper told him. As Sir Jasper spoke, he touched a control panel on one of the arms of his chair, and it smoothly rose a few inches from the floor and began to glide down the stairs. Murph, Mary, Billy, and Hilda followed at a trot to keep up. "We've had to completely reorganize. Lots of new tech to design, of course, which is right up my boulevard. Ah, here we are!"

They had arrived at a large, cluttered workbench near Gertie. "This is my personal workspace," Sir Jasper informed them as Nellie came hurrying over to join them.

"And these are for you." He gestured toward five black wristwatches lying on the table. Their square faces were blank. "Go on, then," he coaxed the Zeroes. "Put 'em on, put 'em on. Don't stand there gaping like haddocks."

Hesitantly they took a watch each and fastened them to their wrists. As they did so, each of the watch faces glowed green and a message appeared in neat lettering: **INITIALIZING.**

Murph glanced quizzically up at Sir Jasper, who gestured for him to keep looking at the watch. Murph saw the message had now changed. **HERO IDENTIFIED**, it read. **KID NORMAL**. The watch gave out a very pleasing little chime. Murph glanced across at Mary's wrist. Her watch face read **MARY CANARY.**

"This is your new, improved HALO communication device!" Sir Jasper declared. "Each one is personally locked on to an individual Hero. Totally hack-proof. The minute it loses contact with your wrist, it'll turn off. So keep them on you when you're on mission standby!"

"And we all get one!" said a delighted Hilda, brandishing her own watch, with the word **EQUANA** picked out in small letters across it. Murph knew she had always been a little miffed that he had been given sole control of their previous HALO unit, which had looked like a black phone.

"Now, come and have a look at this, Master Cooper. I think you'll like it," the old man told him, beckoning him over to the far wall. "We've been doing a bit of work on Carl's old bike."

He led them over to a large shape near his bench and whipped a sheet off the top. A gleaming silvery-blue motorcycle was underneath, with large black wheels and a fat gas tank beneath a long saddle that looked like it could fit all five of them in a pinch.

"Carl was building this for Flora to use on her missions as the Blue Phantom, back in the Golden Age, before Angel went missing," Jasper explained, touching a button on the large control panel on the handlebars. "It's been sitting in that old shed of his since then—he couldn't bring himself to work on it, for one reason or another. Anyway," he continued, coughing elegantly into a silk handkerchief, "I finally persuaded him to bring it here, and now, well, maybe we can actually get it running."

The instrument panel lit up, and a slim row of lights on the front of the bike started flashing from left to right and back again. There was a small beep, and a screen displayed the words WYVERN READY.

"What's a . . . Wivven?" Billy wanted to know.

"*Why*-vern," Jasper corrected him. "It's a kind of dragon. Flora and Carl named the *Banshee* after a screaming ghost because of the whirr of those jets. **And the bike's called the *Wyvern* because, like a dragon . . . it roars."**

He flicked a switch down on the right-hand side of the control panel, and there was a rising whine from the motor.

"Don't stand behind it," Jasper warned Nellie, who was curiously examining the massive twin exhaust pipes on either side. She leaped out of the way as a huge roaring sound erupted from the engine, and licks of flame flashed from the exhausts. The *Wyvern* seemed to be straining on its stand, quivering like a racehorse desperate for the flag.

"Oh, *man*," enthused Nellie, forgetting her customary shyness and running an excited hand over the control panel. "I don't suppose there's any chance—"

"Not a cat's chance in Dogtown, young lady." Sir Jasper smiled. "Not just yet." He shut off the engines and the roaring died away. "She's not quite ready, and I'm sure that old Flora will be the first to give her a spin once she's complete. After all, Carl's been promising her a motorcycle for—hoo, what?—forty years or more, now. So she definitely gets first dibs. Fair?"

"Fair," conceded Nellie reluctantly, giving the beautifully stitched leather saddle a reluctant final slap.

"This looks cool," called Mary. She'd wandered over to the wall, to a rack labeled **MISSION EQUIPMENT:**

74

PROTOTYPES. NOT FOR OPERATIONAL USE.

"What have we got here?"

"What you have got there," answered Jasper, rolling over to her, "is a large, clearly written sign saying, 'Not for Operational Use.' Maybe I should have been even clearer and just put 'Not to be Meddled with by Curious Young Whippers and Snappers.'"

"Oh, come on," wheedled Mary, grabbing a gunmetal-gray box the size of a book from the rack. "What does this do?" She read from a neat sign where it had been stored. "*Dermograph.*"

"Well, if I do say so myself, this little box of tricks is really pretty smart," replied Sir Jasper. "The Dermograph can identify and record all the people in any given area. Watch." He placed the box on the floor and tapped a small button on one corner. There was a rasping whine, and a horizontal beam of light raked around the room. A screen on the Dermograph had now illuminated and was displaying a list of names, including their own. "Very handy if somebody's hiding," Sir Jasper told them. "Not quite mission-ready yet, though." He replaced the box on the rack.

"*Ecto-grenade*," read Billy, looking across the rest of the equipment excitedly, "*Thermo-gun . . . TEMP unit . . .* What's a TEMP unit?"

"Temporary Electro-Magnetic Pulse," explained Sir Jasper. "Knocks out all nearby electrical equipment for three minutes. So do not touch, young Billy. What the Blue Danube is going on now?"

A large green light on the wall had started flashing. **"Ah, the signal! Come on, come on,"** urged Sir Jasper, reactivating his wheelchair and gliding back up the stairs. "It's time for the meeting. Let's go and see what Miss Flint has to say, shall we? Don't dawdle!"

4

A Declaration of War

As they followed Sir Jasper through the stone-paved passageways toward the back of Witchberry Hall, their path became more and more crowded. Squads of Cleaners in their black uniforms, and teams of Heroes they'd never seen before, were all heading in the same direction.

Murph noticed Hilda looking excitedly around her as they moved along, apparently desperate to engage some of their fellow Heroes in conversation. The women and men of the Alliance were mostly chatting among themselves, though. They were dressed more or less normally, but many had bulging muscles clearly visible underneath their clothes, and several carried huge duffel bags and backpacks.

"This is ludicrously awesome," Hilda whispered to him, pointing at one of the bags, which had come slightly open to reveal some kind of silvery metal device. "The actual headquarters of the actual, real, actual, live, Heroes' Alliance! These guys must have been working last night!"

Murph thought back to the news bulletin he had heard on the kitchen radio that morning and wondered whether the team of Heroes marching along beside them had been involved in the flames and bright lights that had lit up the night sky.

They followed the flow through the double doors at the back of the huge house and onto a wide lawn. At the far end was a large dais, and the Heroes and Cleaners were gathering expectantly in front of it. At the back of the stage was a large screen, which was emblazoned with the emblem of the Heroes' Alliance: a stylized letter *H* within a circle.

Miss Flint, the head of the Alliance, appeared, looking immaculate in a smart black suit. She climbed the steps at the back of the dais and began tapping the microphone for silence: **poc-poc!** An expectant hush began to fall across the assembled Heroes.

"Thank you," began Miss Flint—it was the stern kind of "Thank you" that actually means "Be silent immediately." The few remaining pockets of chatter died away.

"Thank you," she said again—but this time the one that actually means "Thank you." "And welcome," she continued, "to the new Alliance base. Our thanks to Sir Jasper for allowing us to use his facility." She waved royally in Jasper's direction, and he lifted a hand in acknowledgment.

"As you know," said Miss Flint, raising her voice slightly, **"the Heroes' Alliance is facing its greatest ever challenge**. Our most dangerous enemy, Magpie—the menace that we were first formed to face—remains at large. We must continue to spare no effort to recapture him as quickly as possible. The very survival of the world of Heroes depends upon it."

There was an anxious murmur. For years, Magpie had been nothing but a dark legend—spoken of only rarely, in hushed tones. Now his presence seemed to hover above the assembled Alliance like a great shadowy bird.

"As well as Magpie," Miss Flint continued, "countless other Rogues remain on the run. But they are scattered and disorganized, and we are working tirelessly to bring them to justice. Only last night, we captured the notorious Yellow Dog, and I am happy to report that he is now back behind bars."

Murph looked automatically across at the burly Heroes he'd first spotted in the corridor and saw that they were high-fiving each other delightedly. Clearly he'd been right—they had been in action last night.

"I want to thank you for everything you have been doing to meet the challenge we're facing," continued their leader. "We have already begun bolstering our numbers, recruiting new Capable Heroes to aid you in the task." Miss Flint raised her voice. **"I want to tell you that there is hope. No matter how beaten down you may feel, how powerless. Because Heroes never surrender. We never give in. We fight without fear."**

She paused for the round of spontaneous applause she'd been expecting at this point to subside.

"Never before have all the members of the Heroes' Alliance been gathered together in one place. But I called you here today for a very important reason. I want you to see the faces of those you are fighting beside. Because the Heroes' Alliance is changing. Two weeks ago Magpie stole my Capability," Miss Flint went on in a softer voice. "I am no longer able to transform into my alter ego, the Glacial Behemoth."

"Ooh," Billy whispered to Murph. "Who knew the giant ice monster had an actual name?"

"Once upon a time, losing my Cape would have forced me to step down from my position as a Hero. **But not anymore!**" Miss Flint shouted. **"I stand and fight with the rest of you!** So, too, does the Blue Phantom!" She gestured to one side, and a ripple of awe ran through the crowd. Standing nearby was the armor-clad figure of a Hero who until recently many in the Alliance had thought was a myth. Murph and the Zeroes were some of the few who knew the Phantom's secret identity—Flora,

The School's mild-mannered secretary and Carl's wife.

"Magpie stole the Phantom's power of invisibility, but that makes her no less of a Hero! And here are yet more Heroes who have suffered at Magpie's hands. They have rejoined the Alliance to make sure he is defeated once and for all!"

Sir Jasper and the rest of his friends—nicknamed the Ex-Cape Committee—were now waving to the crowd. Murph could make out the tall, slim figures of the Gemini Sisters, and the stocky form of Lead Head. Near them stood Carl, with his arm around Angel. She caught Murph's eye and gave a little wave.

"In this most trying of times," Miss Flint was now saying, "we have realized that we can all work together, Cape or no Cape, to fight against evil. And we have one person to thank for this. A young man whose brilliance in the field has taught us an important lesson. The lesson that you don't need superpowers to be a Hero. **I give you . . . Kid Normal!"**

The slight blush that had started building on Murph's face when Angel had waved at him now burst into life like a box of fireworks falling into a volcano on an unusually hot day. Along with Miss Flint, the entire Heroes' Alliance was looking at him and applauding. He felt Mary's hand on his shoulder. His four friends had gathered beside him, facing the crowd.

"Kid Normal and the Super Zeroes!" Miss Flint declared, prompting a fresh fusillade of clapping.

It was the proudest moment of Murph's life so far. Better than the first time flying in the *Banshee*, better than the day the Super Zeroes had become the youngest ever operational Heroes. Face still burning, he felt the applause wash over him like warm bathwater. So many years of not fitting in. So many sleepless hours worrying about whether he would ever make friends. And now here he was—at the helm of the best regarded team of superheroes in the whole of the Alliance. Murph Cooper felt like his happiness roller coaster had reached the very top of its track.

And—unluckily for him—he was right. Because when you reach the top of a roller coaster, you know what happens next, don't you? That's when everything starts to get a bit scary and you wish you hadn't eaten that cotton candy in the line.

There was a sudden burst of static over the speakers, then an earsplitting screech of feedback that made everyone's heads feel like they were being squeezed. The large screen behind Miss Flint flickered, and jagged black lines began to bleed into the picture. Soon the whole screen had been changed to black—and a different emblem now appeared in the center: a silhouette of a bird picked out in stark white.

"Attention . . . Heroes' Alliance,"

said a cruel, mocking voice over the speakers. It sent vines of fear snaking down Murph's back.

"Attention, sneakers in the shadows. Attention, fools."

"It's him," Murph told the others grimly but needlessly. "It's Magpie."

The image of the stark black-and-white bird on the screen had faded away to reveal several people seated at a table. They were lit from behind, so it was hard to make out their faces, but the tall central figure had long straggling hair that Murph and the others couldn't mistake.

"This broadcast is intended for the entire Heroes' Alliance," said Magpie. "And we have a message for you."

The place fell silent as the voice went on.

"You have imprisoned us without trial. You have set yourselves up as judge, jury, and jailer. But your reign of error ends now. We are the Alliance of Evil. We reject you and your ridiculous vow. We declare war on you and all who would support you. We shall wipe you from the surface of this planet and take control."

The silhouetted figures cheered raucously. One of them appeared to be oinking like a pig, but there was no time to puzzle that one out.

"Prepare yourselves for battle, pathetic worms," continued Magpie. "The end is coming."

There was another burst of black-and-white static, and the screen went blank.

If Miss Flint had been taken aback by Magpie's

declaration of war, she didn't show it. **"This changes nothing. We will meet these villains head on, together,"** she told the crowd. But almost before she had finished speaking, HALO units began lighting up.

"Attention, Bobcats," Murph heard a crackly voice say from the wrist of a tall, serious-looking woman nearby. "We have an urgent request from CAMU. Mobilize immediately! We've got reports of Rogue activity at a shopping center."

There was the clatter of booted feet as the Hero and her companions dashed toward Witchberry Hall. Murph could hear what sounded like a police radio transmission being relayed through her HALO unit as they raced past them. *"What on earth is that?"* a crackly voice was saying. ***"It looks like a pig! Call for backup."***

"Massive coordinated Rogue attacks," said Miss Flint's voice over the speakers. "Looks like they're hitting us hard and fast!" She was talking to a Cleaner who'd dashed up to join her on the dais, but the leader of the Alliance had forgotten to turn her microphone off. "Where did this come from? Magpie's always worked alone! **What do you mean, one of them looks like a sponge?"**

There was now complete tumult among the Heroes' Alliance. The sudden realization hit everyone at the same time: the escaped Rogues of Shivering Sands had united behind Magpie to attack them.

"GREAT FRANK ALMIGHTY!" a familiar voice boomed out. *"IT'S WAR! IT'S A GREAT BIG ELEPHANT-SIZED WAR!"*

"Hang on," said Hilda. "Isn't that . . ."

Among the crowd of faces ahead of them was a familiar maroon, bald head. Two small, angry-looking eyes glared above the large red mustache clinging to the nose like a trapeze-swinging fox.

"Mr. Flash!" exclaimed Murph, spinning around.

"COLONEL FLASH, YOU MEAN!" bellowed Mr. Flash at him. *"AND SHUT IT!"*

The Super Zeroes could now see that Mr. Flash— sorry, Colonel Flash—looked a little different from usual. He was still wearing his customary white vest, but he had somehow managed to attach military-style epaulettes to the shoulders, and he bore a row of shining medals on his chest.

"Who made you a colonel?" said Mary, surprise overruling manners.

"I DID!" said Colonel Flash, going a slightly more baroque shade of mauve. "I am a brand-new member of the Heroes' Alliance, and as you know, when you join, you are allowed to select a Hero name. Mine . . . is . . ."

"Colonel Flash, right?" finished Murph for him. He remembered Miss Flint's words about bolstering the numbers and realized that Mr. Flash must have been part of that process.

"About time the Alliance gave me a bit of respect, if you ask me," Colonel Flash was saying to the crowd in general. "A man with huge experience in this field. Someone who is feared and respected in equal measure. Well, maybe a bit more feared, actually." He pondered for a moment. "No, actually more respected. No, hang on—" he stroked his mustache meditatively— "on third thought, I was right the first time. Feared and respected in equal measure."

There was a small collective sigh.

"We're going to have that evil Cape-catcher back behind bars before you know it, sure as eggs is eggs," Colonel Flash went on in a self-satisfied tone.

"SCRAMBLE!" came a sudden voice, apparently from nowhere. Because it came hot on the heels of the egg reference, everyone immediately thought of a plate of delicious, hot scrambled eggs, which was no help whatsoever.

"SCRAMBLE!" came the voice again. Murph realized it was emanating from the HALO device fastened to the Colonel's hairy, puce wrist.

"BLINKIN'
BISCUIT CRUMBS! This is it!" exclaimed Colonel Flash, lifting his arm to see what message he was being sent before performing a surprisingly graceful

pirouette in his excitement. **"HOLY FELT! I'VE BEEN MOBILIZED!"** He blurred and vanished as his superspeed Capability activated.

"Does anyone get the impression he's absolutely loving this?" asked Mary wryly. But there was no time to respond. Because at that moment, the five HALOs attached to their own wrists also crackled into action.

"Super Zeroes! Come in, Super Zeroes! Are you receiving?"

"Super Zeroes receiving," confirmed Murph, lifting the HALO unit to his mouth. "Kid Normal active."

"Take off immediately and investigate potential Rogue activity on a commercial airplane," continued the voice. "Top priority!"

"Get to the *Banshee*," Murph told the others. "Quick!" They began to race back toward the garden where they'd landed.

"Wait up, you guys, wait up!" Murph looked back over his shoulder to see Angel was pelting after them, her silvery hair flying. "Can I come along? Please?"

Murph hesitated. The five Super Zeroes were a tight team. But Angel was the daughter of two of their best friends. They'd just rescued her. It didn't feel right to say no. Involuntarily he glanced across at Mary, who was running beside him. She gave a very slight shake of the head and a purse of the lips. Murph grimaced in a way that was supposed to mean "What can I do?" but just looked like he needed to burp.

"Please?" said Angel again. She had caught up with them by now, and looked around at the Zeroes with an expression of eager friendliness. "Just for the ride, you know? **I'm sick of being cooped up at home! Pleeeeease?"**

"Super Zeroes, are you airborne yet?" came the clipped voice from the HALO. Murph had to make a snap decision.

"Fine. Yes. Let's go," he told her, and the six of them sprinted off together.

5

Ape's on a Plane

Bing! "Good morning, um, ladies and gentlemen, Captain, um, Tim Phillips, here on the flight deck."

The pilot's voice purred over the intercom, following the standard pilot rule of inserting an "um" between every third or fourth, um, word.

"We're now at, um, our cruise altitude of, um, thirty-three thousand feet, with about, um, two hundred miles to go to our, um, destination. Weather, um, pretty good, um, down there. Light, um, breeze, um, um, and, um, scattered, um, cloud, um, cover."

He was starting to overdo the "ums" a bit by this stage, to be honest, and most passengers had put their headphones back on, or were pressing their in-flight entertainment screen to try to get it to work. That included one particularly large, hairy passenger, who was jabbing at the headrest of the seat in front of him with an oversize thumb. He was sitting right at the back of the plane, next to a small man who smelled so bad that everyone assumed the toilet must be blocked.

"So, um, sit back, um, and enjoy the, um, rest of the flight, um . . ." the pilot went on.

"Oh for goodness sake!" squeaked the small man irritably. "Why does this imbecile keep saying 'um'?"

"Malcolm?" said the large man sitting next to him quizzically in a booming voice.

"Never mind, Malcolm," replied his stinky companion. "Just relax and eat your peanuts."

"Malcolm!" replied Malcolm. He began picking handfuls of peanuts out of a large paper bag in his jacket pocket and shoveling them into his oversize red mouth while he idly scratched himself with his other hand.

Malcolm was . . . different from the other people on the plane. For one thing, he was so enormous that his fellow passenger was pushed up against the window. For another, his hairiness was extreme. A shock of bright red hair spilled across the top of his head, so low that it almost touched the clump of hair that rose from underneath his shirt collar. He had huge, wrinkly hands, a snub nose, and large pink ears. In short, he was not unlike an enormous ape—which is one of the reasons he was known as Monkey Malcolm.

The other reason was that if anyone mentioned the word "bananas," he transformed into a real live supercharged ape and went completely . . . well, bananas, for lack of a better word. Don't be alarmed; that's very unlikely to happen. (Yeah, right—look at the title of the chapter. It's totally about to happen.)

On flights such as these, carts packed with snacks and gifts are regularly clattered down the aisles. This breaks up the monotony—not simply because snacking is fun, but also because the cart frequently smacks into the knees of the taller passengers for some additional in-flight entertainment. The one carrying drinks had already careered past Malcolm and his companion, followed by the one bursting with perfume and miniature models of the plane itself (who actually buys those?). Now, as a final treat, the cabin crew were passing through the plane with a cart laden with delicious-looking fruit.

Crunchy apples, refreshing oranges, glistening grapes . . . *Were there any bananas?* we hear you ask. Oh come on, look at the title of the chapter again. Are you not paying attention?

The innocent-looking little fruit cart ground to a halt at the hairy feet at the back of the plane. The smartly dressed lady pushing it began a well-rehearsed speech.

"Okay, got some fruits here for you . . ." she said in a chirpy voice. "Apples, grapes, oranges, ba–"

"NO! NO!" shrieked the little man frantically. **"Don't go on. Stop. Do not go any further."**

"I can't go any further, silly billy, you're at the back of the plane." She wrinkled her nose and gave a quick *sniff-sniff.* "Oh, smells like the toilets are blocked, I'll have a look in a minute after I've gotten rid of all these ba–"

"NO! No! No! No!"

Malcolm's ears had pricked up. "Did you say . . . ?" he began cautiously.

"No, no, don't you worry yourself, Malcolm, all is fine," replied the little man, who then leaned across and hissed intently at the flight attendant, "You must not say the name of the yellow bendies."

"The yellow *what* now? Are you feeling okay, sir?"

"Yes, I'm perfectly fine! Of course I'm fine. Stop looking at me like that. It's very simple. Don't say the name of the fruit that rhymes with *pajamas*. Got it?"

"Well, there's no need to take that tone with me, sir, I was only offering you a . . . 'yellow bendy,' as you call it."

"Well, I don't want one anyway. I hate bananas. **GAH! Look what you made me do!"**

"You said 'bananas'!"

"I know I said 'bananas.' **GAH! I've said it again.** That's twice in ten seconds."

"Three times if you count when I said 'bananas.' That's four now. A whole bunch of bananas. Five! Ha!"

"Stop saying 'bananas'!"

"There you go again—you can't stop yourself! Bananas, bananas, bananas. Bananas! Anyway, is your friend all right?"

At the first mention of bananas, Malcolm had started to swell like a monkey-shaped novelty balloon. Now his already hairy head was erupting with more and more reddish fuzz. There was a ripping noise as his legs burst out of his suit trousers, and within seconds the jacket was torn to pieces as he rose from his seat in full monkey form.

"BEEERRNNAAARRR-NNNERRRS!" roared Monkey Malcolm as the terrified flight attendant did the worst thing possible and raced back up the aisle in terror, still pushing her fruit cart at its top speed and clanging into countless knees as she went.

Spotting the cart full of his favorite food, Malcolm clambered over his companion, and indeed the rest of the row, and bounded up the plane after her. Shrieks and screams began erupting from all parts of the cabin.

"Um, please remain calm, um, ladies and gentlemen, I've been informed that the flight has run into some, um, unexpected monkey back there in the cabin. Um, please don't be alarmed, um, we've contacted the authorities and we're seeking expert advice from them. Until then, sit back, relax if you can, and nobody say 'bananas.' Oh dear."

"BEEERRRNNAAARR-NNNERRRS!" echoed Monkey Malcolm,

finally reaching the fruit cart and scattering its contents with his huge hands. The rest of the passengers crowded to the back of the plane in terror.

"An escaped monkey at thirty-three thousand feet?" exclaimed Mary as Nellie

steered the *Banshee* through a thin layer of cloud.

"Yes, that's what I said, Canary," crackled the voice of Sir Jasper over the radio. "Approach with extra caution. We can't be sure it's Rogue-related, but it's a major coincidence if not. So make sure you neutralize whatever's going on. The passengers are panicking and the pilot sounds like he's losing his cool too— just keeps saying 'um' the whole time."

"Midair rescue!" Mary said excitedly to Murph. "This could be a tricky one."

"Tell me something I don't know." He smiled back at her.

"The dot on top of a letter *i* is called a '*tittle*,'" she replied.

"Huh?"

"You said to tell you something you don't know." Mary sniffed. "There was a lot to choose from, frankly. But I bet you didn't know that."

Murph was forced to admit she was right. He hadn't known that. He couldn't imagine how anyone *would* know that, if he was honest.

"So what's the plan?" Angel said from the back of the cockpit. She was sitting on the floor beside Billy and Hilda, who both looked slightly uncomfortable to have an additional team member all of a sudden.

"We get in there, stop the runaway monkey, and save the passengers," Murph said simply. He was trying to sound cool and devil-may-care, although in fact this sounded like it could turn out to be the most complicated mission the Alliance had handed them to date. But he didn't want Angel to know he was nervous. As she was the daughter of a legendary Hero, he supposed she wouldn't think much of pre-mission butterflies.

"Murph will steer us right, don't worry," Billy told Angel, who raised her eyebrows.

"We're closing in," said Nellie's soft voice as she pointed out a passenger jet in the sky ahead of them. "Prepare for docking."

The *Banshee* drew alongside the plane, and Nellie began one of the most dangerous and complicated maneuvers possible. Carl had trained her well, but she'd never attempted this in a real-life situation. It required all her concentration, complete silence from the other Zeroes, and a full extension of her concentration tongue. Everyone else stuck out their own tongues in sympathy. Feel free to join in. It'll help you concentrate too. We're doing it now as we write.

Metal feet extended from the bottom of the *Banshee* as it turned to face upward and clamped onto the plane using powerful magnets. Everyone except Nellie and Murph, who were strapped into the twin pilots' chairs, had to scramble awkwardly to stand on what used to be the rear wall of the cockpit.

There was a whining noise as the docking procedure took place. The screen in Nellie's control panel showed the message **AIR LOCK SEAL IN PLACE,** and finally a hatch opened up in the *Banshee*'s wall—formerly the floor—revealing the door of the plane just underneath.

"Everybody ready?" said Murph.

"Totally! I love planes!" said Billy. "Can't wait to get on. Maybe I'll get some dinner. Chicken or fish? I especially like that little bread roll you get . . ."

"Everybody ready for the MISSION?" clarified Murph.

"Oh. Yeah, sorry," said Billy sheepishly.

"Monkey first, bread roll second," Mary told him.

"Monkey, right. Yeah, let's go!"

Murph unstrapped himself, dropped down out of his now-upward-facing seat, and knocked on the plane door. He'd never knocked on a plane door before and wasn't sure what the proper thing was. Was there a special midair knock you had to do? But after a moment, the door hissed open and they were greeted by a rather pale-faced flight attendant holding an empty banana peel.

"Hello!" said Murph brightly. "We hear there's some monkey business going on up here?"

"Um, yes, you could say that," replied the traumatized lady. "You'd better, um, come in, I guess." Her day could not get any weirder. She'd spent the past twenty minutes fending off a giant monkey. Six children arriving in a flying car was just the odd icing on an already very strange cake.

The five Super Zeroes, followed by Angel, who looked around curiously, trooped on board the plane.

"Nice plane," she murmured to herself, and Murph realized the last time she had been on a jet was in the 1980s. He had no idea what airplanes had looked like in the last century, but he imagined they'd been made of wood, or something. With ashtrays and possibly chandeliers.

"This is the least hassle I've ever had getting on a flight," piped up Hilda brightly. "We didn't even need to go through security."

"What?" questioned Angel.

"Well, normally it's a nightmare, isn't it? You have to take all the liquids out of your bag . . ."

"Why?" questioned Angel. Murph decided to move things along. There was a great deal for Angel to catch up on, and now was not the time.

"Shall we just agree that it was really easy getting on the flight?" he told the others. "In midair, at five hundred miles an hour, to combat a maniac gorilla."

"Okay," said Hilda, "but still, I didn't even have to check my bag in! I've got knitting needles in here as well!"

"Let's get on with it, shall we?" broke in Mary, who was at the front of the group and had the clearest view of the cabin. "We can all worry about Angel's grasp on modern air travel later, okay?" She spoke breezily, but with a look at Murph that had just a touch of steel in it.

The Super Zeroes and Angel had come in through the rear door of the plane, and as they moved toward the main cabin they could see that the passengers were all crammed into the back, looking anxiously toward the galley area at the front.

"His name's Malcolm," the flight attendant told them, pointing. "He's up there with the fruit cart."

"Traveling in first class? Ooh, someone's doing well," joked Murph.

She looked at him blankly.

"You know what? Never mind," Murph told her. "We'll take a look. Super Zeroes—fold up your tray tables and ensure all seatbacks are in the upright position!"

"What, literally, are you talking about?" Mary snapped at him.

"I don't know, I just get excited on planes, and I've always wanted to say that."

"Ladies and gentlemen," the flight attendant broke in over the speakers. "Please don't be alarmed. We now have some specialist, um, monkey operatives on the flight. Please clear the aisle so they can, um—" she searched for the right word—"de-monkeyfy the plane for us. Thank you."

The passengers crammed into the seats on either side as the Super Zeroes marched confidently toward Monkey Malcolm, who was standing up on one of the front-row seats and rummaging in the overhead bins.

"They're children!" exclaimed one smartly dressed man, looking down his nose at them as they passed. "What on earth are they going to do?"

"You'll be surprised," Mary shot back at him as she

led her friends toward the front. "Although if you want to tackle the giant monkey yourself, please be my guest."

The man harrumphed himself into silence, muttering something about never flying a budget airline ever again. **"Malcolm!"** screeched the huge monkey as they approached, putting down the handbag he'd been chewing on and regarding the new arrivals with suspicion.

"The monkey can talk. Talking monkey," gabbled Billy in alarm. **"Monkey talks."**

"Calm," Murph reassured him.

Mary had moved tentatively forward as far as seat 7C. "Malcolm, is it?" she fluted in what she hoped was a reassuring, measured voice, although in reality it was a trifle high-pitched. "Malcolm the monkey?"

"Monkey Malcolm!" corrected the monkey.

"Come in, Super Zeroes," said a voice from Murph's wrist. "Report mission status."

He lifted his arm and replied, "Super Zeroes receiving. We are on board the plane. And there is

105

indeed a large monkey here. He, ah . . . he says his name is Malcolm."

"Malcolm!" hooted Malcolm.

"Affirmative," came the answer from the Heroes' Alliance. "That's what we thought. Monkey Malcolm is a known Rogue. Petty stuff only, and not an escapee from Shivering Sands. Generally he is harmless, unless anyone mentions the name of the . . . yellow fruit. You know the ones. The ones monkeys like."

Angel, who was standing behind the Super Zeroes, felt a tug on her sleeve. It was the cabin-crew lady. "*Bananas!*" she hissed quietly. "He turned like this right after the man he was with said, 'bananas.' Strange little man."

"Apprehend him and bring him in," the voice from Murph's HALO unit continued. "Try and keep him calm."

Mary nodded. "Would you like to come with us, please, Mr. Monkey Malcolm?" she said in soothing tones. "We really need to give these nice people their plane back. Although some of them aren't that nice," she added under her breath, glancing back over her shoulder at the man she'd mentally nicknamed Mr. Complainy Pants.

106

Monkey Malcolm stepped down from the seat and took a step toward Mary, looking at her curiously. It seemed for a moment as if her soft monkey-touch was working, but suddenly something rather inconvenient happened.

Billy, who was already rather nervous about the prospect of battling a giant monkey, had just discovered a discarded banana peel on one of the seats. (It was 16D, if you're interested—aisle seat on the right. Extra legroom.) He'd picked it up thinking it could be useful as a lure of some kind, but Monkey Malcolm caught sight of it too quickly.

"Ber-NER-NER," he bellowed.

"What, this? No!" squeaked Billy in alarm. Panic made his Cape activate, and with a rasping, trombonesque noise the banana peel suddenly inflated. Billy was now holding a banana peel approximately the size of his own arm.

"BIG ber-ner-ner!"

Monkey Malcolm's eyes widened like those of a monkey child who awakens on monkey Christmas morning to discover that Monkey Santa Claus has come. And it's snowing. Shoving Mary roughly to one side into seat 7F (window), he began to lumber down the aisle toward the others, rapidly gathering speed.

The remaining Super Zeroes scattered to either side as the enormous, slobbering (and, let's not forget, talking) monkey bore down on them—which is something that rarely happens even on budget airlines.

"Billy! Throw the peel!" yelled Murph as he dived into row 12 to avoid being trampled.

"What?" queried Billy, who for a split second thought Murph was trying to invent a new slang term for shaking hands.

"Throw . . . the peel! Under his feet!" urged Murph as Monkey Malcolm careened past him like a hairy train. **"NOW!"**

Just as the ape was about to slam into him, Billy hurled the peel like a giant novelty Frisbee given away to the delegates at an international banana conference. It landed neatly under Monkey Malcolm's feet as Billy threw himself to the left (across row 16, seats A, B, and C).

Monkey Malcolm surfed down the aisle on the

peel, windmilling his arms and still accelerating. The passengers scattered to either side as he slid past them and, with a resounding *clang*, knocked himself out on the toilet door at the back of the cabin.

"All right, all right, I'm nearly finished," came a quavering voice from inside the toilet.

Malcolm slowly fell over backward. He was snoring large, banana-scented snores even before his head hit the carpet.

The toilet door opened and a tiny old lady peeked out. "What's all this commo–" she began, before seeing the huge ape on the floor. "Ooh dear, someone's had a bit too much to drink, haven't they," she muttered crossly to herself as she stepped over him, flicking her hands dry.

"It is now safe for you to move about the cabin," Murph told the passengers perkily. "The captain has switched off the giant-monkey sign." Many of them looked at him blankly, but they gradually began to file back to their seats.

"Come on," Murph told the others as he shouldered his way through the crowd to join them. "Grab a monkey limb each! **Let's get him**

back to the Alliance before he wakes up."

Angel joined them as they began to drag the still-snoring ape toward the *Banshee.* "What about the other man?" she asked Murph.

He looked at her quizzically. Mary spoke up: "What other man? What are you talking about?"

"Well . . ." said Angel, "the cabin-crew lady said there was another man. A strange little man, she said. So Malcolm had someone with him."

Mary wrinkled her nose, partly because she was irritated at having missed this information herself, and partly because she now realized there was a hideous smell at the back of the plane. "What *is* that revolting smell?" she asked the others, as they dumped Monkey Malcolm into the *Banshee*, where he landed with a soft *thud.*

"It smells like a trash can . . . that's gone bad. And been put in another can," said Hilda. "A can in a can."

"A can in a can?" queried Murph.

"A can in a can," confirmed Mary. It was beginning

to sound like a tongue twister, but luckily the cabin-crew lady cut in before things got too funky.

"I thought it smelled like garbage too! That's what I said to that funny man who was sitting next to the monkey."

"What funny little man?" said Murph sharply.

"Told ya!" Angel added.

"He was a strange guy," she answered. "Didn't want me to say, 'bananas.' Got very snippy when I brought the fruit around."

"Where is he," asked Murph. "Can you see him?"

She looked around at the passengers, who were gradually retaking their seats, chattering excitedly. "No, can't see him anywhere now . . ." She pondered. "That's weird."

"Murph," said Hilda, muffling her words by stretching her mouth out as far as it could go. "Look over here." It sounded more like *"Rook rover rear"* but Murph managed to crack the code. "In da drash," Hilda continued.

"*In da drash*? What?"

"IN . . ." said Hilda sharply, getting out one of her knitting needles and gesturing toward a large black trash bag that was sagging on the floor at the back of the jet, "da DRASH!" At this, she poked the needle sharply into the bag.

There was a sharp cry of **"Whaaaargh!"** then a silence.

Murph walked up to the trash bag and coughed politely. "Is there somebody in there?"

"No," replied the trash bag firmly.

"Well, who said that, then?"

"Nobody. Just . . . an empty chips bag rustling and sounding a bit like human speech. **Crrrrrsk Crrrrrsk** salt and vinegar."

"Chips bags don't talk," Murph told the bag, "and if they did, they wouldn't just name their own flavor. Come out of there!"

"Sour cream and onion . . ." wailed the voice desperately. "Yowch! Stop it!" Hilda had plied her knitting needle once again. The top of the bag opened, and DoomWeasel's head emerged with a cardboard coffee cup perched on top like a moist party hat. Dribbles of cold coffee trickled down each cheek. "Oh, hello," he greeted them lamely.

"Mr. Drench!" exclaimed Billy, understandably flabbergasted to see his ex-CT-teacher-turned-manic-rubbish-obsessed-Rogue popping out of a trash bag thirty-three thousand feet in the air. **"I don't believe it!"**

"I am Mr. Drench no longer!" insisted the little man, bursting out and doing a mad little capering dance in the aisle. "I am DoomWeasel! Although I did have to check in for this flight under my original name. But that is of no matter! **For I am DoomWeasel and I am—"**

"Coming with us," said Hilda firmly, pointing her knitting needle at him like a fencer. "The Heroes' Alliance has some questions for you, mister. And for your monkey friend too!"

She herded the little man like an armed sheepdog through the back door and into the *Banshee*. "Sit down quietly next to Malcolm," she told him. "One false move, and I'll crochet you." Billy joined her to keep watch over the prisoners as Nellie climbed up into the pilot's chair, still facing upward like an astronaut, and began to prepare for take-off.

Back on the plane, Mary and Murph were looking at each other in amazement. "Did we just—on the first day of the war—capture Magpie's main henchman?" Mary asked, widening her eyes and holding up her hand ready for a high five.

"Thanks to me, you did," Angel interrupted, appearing between them and slapping Mary's upraised hand delightedly. "Didn't think to check for extra Rogues, did you? Maybe I should come on all your missions, huh? Help you out? I'll talk to Mom about it. **Come on, guys, let's bounce!"**

She swanned off through the rear door, leaving Murph and Mary alone together once again. "Actually, she's right," Murph said wryly.

Mary spluttered slightly. "We . . . we *would* have checked! We would!"

Murph raised his eyebrows wordlessly.

"We would have noticed the smell. We wouldn't have let Drench slip through our fingers," Mary told herself as she turned away and climbed out through the plane door.

"Please sit back, relax, and enjoy the rest of the flight!" Murph told the passengers, who looked at him nonplussed as he followed Mary, the cabin-crew lady closing the door behind them.

"Come in, Alliance," said Murph into his HALO. "Flight eighty-three is now ape-free. I've got no idea how you're going to explain that one away."

"We'll think of something," came a voice from his wrist. "Depressurization. Hallucinations. We'll wing it."

"Very good," Murph replied, bursting with excitement at what he was about to say. "And . . . we got a bonus as well. We also have DoomWeasel in custody."

"Thanks to me!" called Angel in the background.

There was a slight pause before the message came back. "DoomWeasel? That's amazing work! Are you sure?"

Murph pinched his nose. "Pretty sure. Please have Cleaners standing by at Witchberry Hall. And also . . . cleaners. Actual people who clean. The *Banshee's* going to need a good old wipe."

"Detaching!" cried Nellie at the controls. The *Banshee* undocked itself from the side of the jet and roared off back the way it had come.

6

Murph's Missions

The following morning, Murph walked to school like a frolicsome young giraffe on its way to a long-neck competition. He was riding high. Not only had the Super Zeroes completed their mission, they had given the Heroes' Alliance a valuable prisoner—someone who must know the inner workings of Magpie's Alliance of Evil.

DoomWeasel had been taken away by a squadron of Cleaners as soon as they'd landed back at Witchberry Hall. **"I will never talk! I will never wash! I am all-powerful!"** he had squeaked as he was led away. Murph wasn't particularly confident that the Alliance would be able to get much useful information out of him. But at least he was behind bars.

Thanks to me, Angel's voice sounded in his head. And Murph was forced to admit that she was right. They had been so excited to capture Monkey Malcolm, it had never occurred to any of them to check for hidden accomplices. It was thanks to her that the midair mission had turned from a mere success into something of a triumph.

He pondered Angel's request to come along on more of their adventures and found the thought far from unpleasant. Sure, Mary seemed a little put out, but Murph was sure she'd get over it. After all, nobody had ever said the Super Zeroes could only have five members.

The war against the Alliance of Evil had started with a major victory for their side, and Murph was feeling buoyant. Surely it would all be over by Christmas. But as soon as he turned onto the nondescript side street where The School was located, he realized the threat from Magpie was being taken very seriously indeed.

A line of sandbags topped with barbed wire had been constructed outside the main gates, and several figures in black were visible ahead.

As Murph approached, a woman with a stroller hurried past him in the opposite direction, looking pale and scared. **"Don't go that way!"** she called over her shoulder to him as she fled. **"It's not safe!"**

The school gates were being guarded by several Cleaners, who were checking the identity of students on large green HALO units as they filed through a gap in the barricade. "Morning!" Murph said to one of them as he squeezed through. "Not sure what you said to that lady, but she's certainly in a hurry to get away!"

"Told her we've got an escaped tiger cornered in here," he answered.

"What?"

"Well, we can't just keep saying 'gas explosion,' can we? Used that excuse sixteen times yesterday alone, what with all the fighting going on. We had a shopping center trashed . . . all kinds of chaos. Don't know how we're going to keep a lid on all this, to be honest with you."

Murph had never encountered such a talkative Cleaner before. Normally they were tight-lipped and serious. Apparently the pressure of keeping an entire war secret from most of the population had broken through that customary reserve.

"Now that you come to mention it though, maybe an escaped tiger is a bit alarming," he continued, "in a school. Yes . . . maybe we'll tone it down a bit . . . Escaped . . . I dunno . . . goat, or something."

Mrs. Fletcher, the school librarian, was standing just inside the gates, urging the students to hurry inside. **"Quick, quick, PAAAAARP!"** she encouraged them—her Capability briefly activating and her head morphing into a foghorn, as per usual. "You never know who might be lurking. There are Rogues everywhere . . . **PAAAAAARP!"**

A lady whose head turns into a foghorn is, perhaps, not the ideal choice to keep everyone calm. But there was a war on, and everyone was "doing their bit."

More sandbags were piled up beside the main doors to The School, and extra cameras had been installed overlooking the schoolyard.

In the entrance hall, Mr. Flash was pinning up a large poster. Today his military-style garb was topped off with an olive-green helmet covered in webbing.

"KEEP MOVING, KEEP MOVING! DON'T YOU KNOW THERE'S A WAR ON?" he bellowed at Murph, who had stopped to read the poster.

"Did you, um . . . did you design the poster yourself, Mr. Flash?" Murph asked innocently.

"COLONEL FLASH, YOU CHAFFINCH!" replied the teacher. "And, yes, I did, as a matter of fact."

There was a pile of other posters at his feet. Murph turned his head sideways to read the next one, which announced:

KEEP
CLAM
AND
CARRY
ON

"Are you sure this is spelled right?" he asked.

"SHUFF UFF," mumbled the teacher through a mouthful of thumbtacks.

"Hope your Alliance mission went well," Murph said, to try and mollify him. At this, the teacher's eyes lit up. Spitting the tacks out into a ham-like hand, he adjusted his medals proudly.

"Don't know why they didn't bring me in years ago," he told Murph gruffly. "Total success. Slight collateral damage to a shopping center, but there you go. There's a war on! No point in mimbling in there like a shy sprout. You need to strike hard, fast, and hard!" He slammed a fist into his open palm to illustrate this, wincing as several thumbtacks pierced his knuckles.

"Seventeen separate Rogue attacks since the war broke out, I heard," Mr. Flash went on, turning back to the wall and beginning to pin up a poster reading:

CARELESS TALK COSTS HEROE'S, SO SHUT IT!

The errant apostrophe was bothering Murph, but not as much as another thought which had begun to buzz around his brain. He thought back to Magpie as he had first seen him, pacing restlessly around his underwater cell. The man in black had usually worked alone—only using other Rogues like DoomWeasel when they could be of use to him. This sudden formation of an entire army just didn't seem right. What was he planning?

As Murph turned away from Mr. Flash and began to move toward the auditorium for the assembly, he was unable to shake the uncomfortable feeling that unseen eyes were watching him. Dark eyes, full of hatred and cunning. If Magpie used others only for his own ends, Murph pondered, why start a war? To keep both the Alliance and the escaped Rogues busy fighting each other while he plotted . . .. what? Murph shivered, as if invisible wings had stirred the air around him into a chill breeze.

As Murph hurried along toward the cafeteria a few hours later, he spotted Carl on a stepladder, screwing a set of metal bars onto one of the large ground-floor windows. "Not that it'll stop Rogues from getting in," he was muttering to himself. "Waste of time, if you ask me. Makes the place look like a prison. Ah, Captain Brush!" he added as he saw Murph. "Just the man I wanted to see! Got time for a cup of tea?"

Together, they left through the back doors of The School, passing another wartime poster reading "YOUR COUNTRY NEEDS ME" below a hand-drawn picture of Mr. Flash.

"I hear young Angel was a good addition to the team?" asked Carl, his breath condensing in the chilly air as they trudged across the frosty playing fields toward his workshop.

YOUR COUNTRY NEEDS

ME

"Yeah," Murph confirmed, feeling a warm glow at the old man's pride in his daughter.

"Very nice," Carl went on. "Yes, lovely." He seemed a little awkward and almost embarrassed as he added, "Got a favor to ask you, actually."

"Oh yes?"

"Yes. Tell you about it inside. Ah, here we are."

They had arrived at the wooden door of the ramshackle collection of huts and garages that stood at the top of a steep slope near the edge of the woods. Carl turned the handle, calling out "We're here, dearest!" as he led Murph inside.

Carl's workshop was Murph's favorite part of The School. The main room, with its creaking floor of wooden planks, was a reassuring jumble of workbenches, with the pleasing, warm smell of oil and paint. Low winter sun streamed in, illuminating floating motes of dust and reflecting back from the silvery hair of the two people sitting in armchairs near the windows.

Murph was struck for the first time by how alike Angel and her mother were. They had been chatting contentedly as Murph and Carl came in, each unconsciously mirroring the other, sitting with their legs crossed and their arms folded. Angel had been chuckling at something, her eyes creased into laugh lines that would, in time, fold into the kindly wrinkles that had smiled at Murph many times over the past year.

"What's up, Coops?" cried Angel.

"Ah, here he is!" Flora welcomed him. "Come on, sit down, sit down. Angel's just been telling me all about your airborne monkey business yesterday."

"She was great," Murph said truthfully as he slumped into one of the chairs opposite them. Flora reached out and patted her daughter's knee.

"We had a fairly interesting day ourselves," said Carl from the workbench, where he was bustling around making tea underneath the shelf with its mismatched collection of angel statues—one for each year they'd believed their daughter was dead. "Got sent off on a mission. Well, I mean most of us did, what with the Alliance of Evil mounting so many attacks at the same time. Great to see Flora in action again," he added, clinking teaspoons.

"Not quite the same without my invisibility," Flora said. "I used to be able to sneak up on a Rogue, then—**_bam!_** Hit them with the old roundhouse kick."

Carl laughed. "The Cape might have gone, but the kick's still very much intact! Don't think that pig knew what hit him." He brought steaming mugs over to the chairs and eased himself down with a grunt into the final battered leather armchair.

"Nice to be wanted even without a Cape, though," mused Flora. "The Alliance has changed a lot—thanks to you, young man." Murph did a little light blushing.

"And I was glad to be out and about too," Angel said cheerfully. "Sitting around the house is mega-dullsville."

"I think a slight period of adjustment was in order, dear," Flora told her. "After all, you've had thirty whole years to catch up on."

"I know, I know," said Angel resignedly. "You've told me, like, a squillion times. Take it slowly, you're not ready, we don't fully understand your Cape yet, yadda yadda yadda."

Murph pricked his ears up at this. He had been curious about Angel's Capability ever since the day the Zeroes rescued her from Magpie's secret laboratory. She'd shot two bright beams of light that had saved them from the ice monster the Rogue transformed into.

He remembered thinking, with a slight pang of envy, what a cool power it was.

"What's wrong with your Cape? Is there a problem with those light beams or something?" he asked now.

"There certainly is," Carl replied. "The problem is . . . that's not her Cape! At least, it wasn't . . ."

Murph was dumbstruck for a moment. "I don't follow you," he said, crinkling his brow.

"Her Cape was invisibility, like her mom," said Carl simply. "We'd been trying to train her, because it . . . well, it didn't seem to work properly, you see. Some days she could go invisible, some days she couldn't. It's only in the past few days that Angel's been able to tell us what was really going on."

"Which is what, exactly?"

"Maybe it's best if we tell you what happened the night she disappeared," Carl said softly. **"THIRTY YEARS AGO . . ."**

We're off to the past again! Woo-hoo! Ready? It's time to climb aboard the magical time-travel cat. Hold on tight, because it's a flying time-traveling cat, and it's just been cleared for takeoff by feline air traffic control. Five . . . four . . . three . . .

Oh, hang on, it's sitting down next to the radiator. Get up, magical time-travel cat! Stop licking yourself! We need to get on with the story. That's better. Right . . .

What now, time-travel cat? You want to sit in a cardboard box for three hours? There isn't time! No, you can't have any cheese, it's bad for you. Let's go.

Fly, magical cat, fly! To the past! Wheeeeeeeee!

SCENE: THE PAST

"Right, Angel love, let's try again, shall we? Concentrate!" Flora Walden tied up her long, silvery hair and smiled encouragingly at her daughter.

Angel stood on the hearth in the living room of the Waldens' little stone cottage. A cheerful fire bubbled and snapped in the grate, sending homey golden shadows flicking across the comfortable room. She bent her knees slightly and concentrated, beads of sweat forming on her brow. After a few seconds, she let out her breath with a frustrated trumpet.

"It's no good, Mom, I just can't do it! It's gone!"

"It can't have 'gone,' Angel. Once a Cape appears it can't just disappear!"

"Well, neither can I, apparently. Not today at least." Angel flumped herself down into a well-stuffed armchair and puffed out her cheeks.

"I just don't understand it, love," said Flora sadly, leaning on the back of the chair. "Yesterday night you went invisible, just like that! Pop! Gone! Not even a ripple in the air! I mean, even I can't do it that smoothly. But today, you can't seem to do it."

"It's not fair!" huffed her daughter—the 2,278,312th use of this phrase by a teenager in the year 1988 alone. Angel actually stamped her foot on the carpet in frustration, sending the cat scuttling out of the room in fright. (It's not the time-travel cat; it's a different cat.)

"Angel, I know you want to be a Hero, but we can't risk exposing you before you're ready," soothed Flora.

"But I AM ready," snapped Angel. **"I couldn't be more ready."**

Her mother's face softened. "I know you're impatient, my love. But it's for the best." Angel turned away from her toward the fire.

A door at the back of the living room burst open, admitting a cloud of smoke. A figure in thick leather gloves and a huge metal mask was standing in the doorway. "What's all the shouting in here?" boomed a metallic voice from behind it.

"Oh, hello, love," answered Flora mildly. "You been working on the suit?"

The figure in the doorway pushed back the welder's mask, revealing a flushed pink face underneath a mop of thick brown hair. "Yeah, just fixing your helmet," Carl replied. "That cannonball put quite a dent in it. Taken me half an hour to hammer it out."

"Yes, well," mused Flora, "at least Blue Peter's safely locked away now. That new prison out at sea seems to be working. And there's a special cell reserved in there for Magpie."

"Which is exactly why I want to help catch him!" burst out Angel from her place by the fire. "Dad, can't you have a word with her? I'm a teenager! I can't stay cooped up in this cottage forever!"

There was a sudden clatter of rotor blades from the dark garden. Red and green lights flashed through the kitchen window at the back of the cottage. "What on earth does he want at this time of night?" fussed Flora, peering out.

"Well, I don't think he's delivering pizza, let's put it that way," quipped Carl.

There was a knock at the back door, which burst open almost immediately to reveal a tall, athletic-looking man with wavy hair and a small, neat black beard. "Hello, hello!" he said to the room at large.

"Evening, Jasper," answered Flora calmly. "What's up?"

"Treasons, stratagems, and spoils, old cabbage!"

replied Sir Jasper Rowntree. "How's that dent in the old coal scuttle?"

"Carl just fixed it."

"Splendid! Well, pop it on and let's go!" said the man in the doorway excitedly. "Got a lead!"

"Hang on, hang on," answered Carl. "You mean you've got a lead . . . on Magpie?"

"Could be," Sir Jasper answered. "I've been going back over the latest missing Hero reports, and something looks fishy to me about the spot where one of the disappearances happened. Worth taking a gander, I'd say. Come on, come on! Gertie's getting impatient!"

Flora turned to Angel. "Will you be all right, love, if we—"

"Go off and fight evil and leave me here with nothing to do?" she replied bitterly.

Sir Jasper concentrated for a second, and the TV in the corner of the room turned itself on. "There you go, young missy!" he told her. "Your favorite Australian soap-based drama is just about to start, I daresay."

Angel, furious at being told to content herself with the television while her parents went on the hunt for a supervillain, threw herself back down into the armchair and refused to say goodbye to either of them as the sound of the *Banshee*'s jet engines fired up from the garage next door, mingling with the clattering of Sir Jasper's heli-car.

As the engine noise died away, Angel sighed petulantly. She hated being left behind. Then the thought struck her . . . Why *did* she have to be left behind? Would a true Hero sit idly by while others flew into action? She smiled a determined smile to herself, stood up, and marched through to the deserted garage.

There were scorch marks on the concrete floor from the flying car's engines, and the open doors were admitting a chilly breeze, but Angel ignored it. In one corner of the room was an old wooden desk littered with notebooks and paper. She had seen her parents sit here, hour after hour, poring over their documents, trying desperately to work out where Magpie was operating from. Pinned up above the desk was a map on which Carl had neatly written "*Missing Heroes*." It was covered with yellow sticky notes, each bearing a date and a set of coordinates written in her father's neat penciled handwriting.

Angel scanned the notes, looking for the most recent. They were widely scattered across the whole country—Magpie was proving extremely difficult to pin down. But, she noticed, one of the notes bearing a recent date had a question mark drawn in the corner. That must be it! That must be where they had gone. Well, Angel thought to herself, ripping the note from the map, it was time to give them some backup. She imagined herself arriving at a crucial point in the mission, and helping her parents out. How surprised they'd be!

Still holding the note, Angel marched over to a large, bulky shape in the corner of the garage, shrouded in an oil-spattered white sheet. She grabbed a corner of the sheet and threw it back, revealing a slim, silvery motorcycle, gleaming in the track lighting hanging from the ceiling. A handwritten note was fastened to the instrument panel at the front. It read:

FUNCTIONAL PROTOTYPE. EXPERIMENTAL. DO NOT USE UNDER ANY CIRCUMSTANCES. ANGEL, THIS MEANS YOU.

Nobody ever got to be a Hero by paying attention to signs, thought Angel to herself, ripping the note off and crumpling it in her right hand as, with her left, she flicked a large switch in the center of the panel.

There was a deep hum, coupled with a high-pitched whining from the motorcycle's engine. A screen lit up

in the center of the handlebars, and pixelated letters spelled out the words **ENTER COORDINATES**.

Angel punched in the numbers from the sticky note on a keypad beside the screen. The whine from the engines rose to a scream, and the message on the screen changed.

COORDINATES ACCEPTED, the green letters now read. **HOLD ON**.

Angel clung tightly to the handlebars as the motorcycle chugged toward the doors. Once it was out underneath the stars, there was a *clunk* as the two large cylinders on either side of the fuel tank opened up. Angel gasped in surprise and delight as a pair of slim, silver wings extended in front of her knees, and the whole bike began to shake. There was a cough and splutter as the engines warmed up, followed by a roar louder than a hundred of those hand dryers you get in public toilets that are far too loud. Angel let out an involuntary whoop of mingled fear and excitement as the jets fired with a lick of flame from each exhaust pipe and the *Wyvern* shot upward into the night sky.

An hour later, the *Wyvern* skidded to a halt in a large, bare hangar. Angel pried her hands from the handlebars and wiped the sweat from her brow. It had been a thrilling flight underneath the stars, right until the bike had aimed itself directly at an enormous concrete dam blocking off the end of a wide valley. Only when it seemed she was about to crash into a waterfall had she noticed the hangar entrance behind it, and the bike—its screen now saying **LANDING SITE IDENTIFIED**— had steered itself through.

There was no sign of the *Banshee* or of Gertie. Perhaps her parents and Jasper had landed somewhere else, she thought to herself as she explored. A small blinking light, next to a set of doors set in one of the metal walls, caught her attention. So this place wasn't completely deserted, at least! Angel moved across to the doors and pressed a button. They slid smoothly open, revealing an elevator, and without hesitation she stepped inside.

When the elevator doors opened once again at the bottom of the shaft, Angel stepped out into a huge, dimly lit laboratory. Flashing banks of monitors were piled on workbenches here and there. A glass structure, like an enormous birdcage, was hanging above a large control panel, hooked up to it by thick black wires. And at the other end of the room, on top of a slim metal plinth, a small silvery box pulsated with flashing lights. The whole place seemed empty; it was silent except for the deep hum of the equipment and her own excited breathing.

A secret lab! Surely this was useful information to take back to her parents, even if they weren't here after all. A quick hunt for clues, and she could leap back on the *Wyvern* and be home in time to surprise the Blue Phantom with the news that her daughter *was*, undeniably, mission-ready.

Angel moved forward softly toward the nearest bank of equipment, but almost immediately froze. A small, low door had hummed open at the far end of the room and a man dressed in an expensive-looking black coat had stepped through. He had long hair streaked with white and a beaked nose. Magpie! Could it really be him? Angel had heard all the stories about the man in black—the man who could steal other people's Capabilities. Ducking behind the workstation, she tensed herself, all her senses suddenly heightened. Now more than ever, she needed to activate her erratic power. If she could make herself invisible, then maybe she would be able to sneak out unnoticed.

Scrunching up her face in concentration, Angel tried with all her might to disappear. But, looking down, she was horrified to see that she was far from invisible. In fact, she was the opposite of invisible.

She was visible. Incredibly, frighteningly visible. In ultra high definition.

"What on earth are you doing?" came the man's calm, curious voice. He had circled around, silent as a cat on his feet, and was watching her intently.

Angel realized she had been wiggling her fingers in front of her face, to see if they were at least becoming slightly transparent. She dropped her hand and entered a combat stance, trying to stop her legs from shaking with fear. She was in no doubt now—this was Magpie. Somehow, by chance, she'd stumbled into one of his secret bases.

Magpie drank in her terror like a milkshake. "Lost your mommy and daddy?" he mocked her. "How very, very sad."

Angel desperately tried to bluff. "My mom's on her way," she told him. "And you'd better run. The Blue Phantom will make mincemeat out of you."

"The Blue . . . Phantom?" breathed Magpie, taking a step closer to her. "The Blue Phantom is . . . your mother?"

"Yes," said Angel bravely.

Magpie clapped his hands in delight. "Oh, how delicious!" Suddenly his eyes widened with greed. "And tell me, young lady, what is the Capability you were trying so hard to activate just now? Do you have the same ability as your mother? That rarest of all gifts . . . invisibility?"

Angel's eyes brimmed, and Magpie crowed with delight. "Splendid! I've heard many stories about the Phantom, but I never realized she had a daughter with the same Capability! That makes things much more convenient." His eyes narrowed to a pair of vicious slits, and he jabbed his hands toward Angel, who was suddenly surrounded by a web of purple lightning. She stumbled.

But Magpie's cry of triumph died on his thin lips.

"What's going on?" he muttered to himself furiously. "There's no superpower here to steal!" The purple energy bolts dissolved into the air. "You don't have the power of invisibility. You have no Capability at all!"

Angel was confused. She knew this wasn't true—

she *did* have the power to make herself invisible . . . sometimes. It certainly wasn't working today, though.

To buy herself some time, she dived behind the nearest workbench, aiming to get as far away from Magpie as possible.

She furrowed her brow and thought frantically. "Oh no you don't!" he bellowed, activating one of his stolen Capes. He held out his hands, palms first, and shot two bright white beams of light at the bench, toppling it over backward.

Angel instinctively flung her arms forward to stop the bench from falling on her. But as she did so, there was a flash, and two beams of energy shot out of her own hands. She was forced to screw up her eyes—the lights were incredibly bright, more intense by far than the ones Magpie had produced. There was an electric sizzle as they cut through the air, narrowly missing her enemy, and

slammed into the far wall in a shower of white-hot sparks.

Magpie bellowed in rage and fright as he ducked out of the way. Angel was staring down at her hands, dumbstruck. **I copied him,** she thought to herself in wonder. **I copied his Cape!** And then it hit her. *That* was why she'd sometimes been able to become invisible. It had been the times that Flora had disappeared *first*—to show her how it was done. Her Capability wasn't invisibility at all! It was the power to copy other people's Capes! And—if those intense beams were anything to go by—her versions were even more powerful than the originals.

A similar train of thought seemed to have occurred to Magpie. He was slowly backing away from her, an expression of combined fear and wonder on his face.

He's on defense, Angel thought to herself. *Time to press my advantage. I need to attack.*

She sprinted toward the man in black, full of confidence and ready to return whatever fire he tried to throw at her. It was only when she was halfway across the space between them that she saw his expression twist from one of fear to one of cruel mockery.

"So brave," he said to her. "And such a unique Capability. I need some time to work out what to do with you, Little Miss Cape Magnifier."

He shot out another blast of the white energy beams—and although they seemed thin and weedy compared to her own, Angel had to stop to duck out of the way. She quickly gathered herself, though, and prepared to strike. She now knew that she could produce her own beams to mimic Magpie's—and she launched herself into a flying kick, preparing to unleash them.

Magpie was grinning now, a grimace without any joy in it. "Luckily," he said as Angel jumped, "you've put yourself just where I want you."

Magpie had backed away to lure Angel beneath the glass cage suspended from the ceiling. While she was in midair, he slammed his fist down onto a button. There was a whine of machinery, a jet of steam, and the cage full of eerie reddish light dropped suddenly, trapping Angel inside.

"And the next thing I remember," Angel told Murph now, "was the cage breaking, and that ice monster pegging it toward me, roaring. So I just . . . let rip . . ."

"With the light beams you'd copied from Magpie thirty years earlier!" Murph completed for her. He took a sip of tea and realized that while he'd been engrossed in the story it had crossed the line from nice and warm to really hideous old-dishwater temperature.

"Magpie was clever," said Flora. "He moved the *Wyvern* to his main base at the Scarsdale quarry so we'd never know where he had trapped Angel. We tracked it there."

"And that's when we got all the Heroes together, basically," Carl summarized. "When we faced off with Magpie and he blew up the quarry, there was no reason for us to doubt that Angel . . . had been inside." He bustled off to the workbench with the teacups, reaching a hand up, apparently to adjust his checked cap.

"Angel, love, go and help your dad out, will you?"

said Flora gently. Angel moved over to Carl and helped him take the tea things through to the garage next door.

"We wanted you to know all this," Flora said to Murph, quietly and seriously, "because it's Angel's first day at The School. With the war going on, Mr. Souperman wants all Capable students to be trained as quickly as possible. But this is all very new to her. When Magpie imprisoned her, there were no special schools for people with Capes, there was no Heroes' Alliance. Heroes worked alone. And no matter how she might try and seem casual, it's all a bit scary."

Murph nodded, imagining what it must feel like to miss thirty years.

"I may be getting a bit old now, but I've been this school's secretary for decades and I know what kids can be like," Flora went on. "I need you to promise me something. I need you to keep Angel safe and happy here. Don't let her feel left out. Don't let the other students bother her. Do you think you can do that?"

"I absolutely can," said Murph, without hesitation holding out a hand for Flora to shake.

"Good man," said Carl's voice. Murph

turned to see that the janitor had come back through from the garage and had obviously heard the end of the conversation. "Flora and I knew you wouldn't let us down. I know you'll take care of my Angel. We're both counting on you."

"Let me make sure I've got this absolutely, completely straight," said Mr. Geoffrey Souperman ten minutes later. **"You want me to stage a fake . . . Parents' Night? Next Thursday?"**

On his way back from Carl's huts, Murph had suddenly remembered that he needed to get this organized, and he went straight to the principal's office, his head beginning to spin a little from all of the different tasks he was juggling. His mom had asked again about Parents' Night the previous night, and then at breakfast that morning she had actually offered to telephone The School herself to find out the details.

Mr. Souperman sighed, looking at Murph as if he was an especially painful pimple in an unusually tender place. "And you are aware, are you not," the principal asked him, "that there's a war on?"

"Sorry," said Murph quite truthfully. "Honestly, if there was any other way, I'd take it. But she's a fairly determined lady."

"Very well," snapped Mr. Souperman, seeming to decide that it was better to rip off the Band-Aid of embarrassment, rather than peel it excruciatingly away. "Tell your mother to report for Parents' Night at . . . oh, I don't know"—he wheeled around and consulted the clock on his desk—"seven a.m. I'll get some of the teachers to mock something up. And you're sure this will allay her suspicions?"

"Sorry," Murph said tentatively. **"Parents' Night will be . . . next Thursday morning?"**

"Yes," snapped the principal. "There's no way we can admit a non-Capable person to school premises after dark, not with so many Rogues at large. The whole grounds are patrolled by a squad of Cleaners from dusk until . . . ah, until early morning. Bring your mother here before classes start on Thursday, seven a.m. sharp. That should suffice, eh?"

"Oh, yes," said Murph, trying to sound more confident

than he felt. "If she sees it's just a normal school, she'll totally forget all about it."

There was the sound of a distant explosion, and they both looked out of the window to see a third-year girl running across the playing fields, pursued by what appeared to be a large walking bush. They both heard a distant shout of **"Hey! No Capes during lunch break, Natasha! Transform back this instant."**

"A normal school," repeated Mr. Souperman drily.

"Yes. Well, fake Parents' Night first thing on Thursday morning, then. What could possibly go wrong?"

Murph backed out of the room, grinning nervously.

7

Raft Rift

Looking back later, Murph realized that the CT lesson on Wednesday morning was the point at which everything started to go wrong. Lots of other things went much wronger later on, but this was the beginning of it all—the wobbling wheel that sent the go-kart of his life careening toward the unfenced sewage farm of destiny.

Of course, it happened on a Wednesday—the day all truly bad things tend to happen. And as usual, it was one teacher in particular who was the harbinger of doom. Mr. Flash had a nice hot helping of doom ready for Murph Cooper, and he was ready to harbinge the heck out of it.

Murph hadn't managed to tell the rest of the Super Zeroes about Angel and her Capability yet. His mind had been taken up with worries about Parents' Night taking place on Thursday morning and whether there was any chance at all that his mom would find The School even a tiny bit normal.

He'd been intending to talk them through it as they all arrived for Capability Training that morning—CT was always the first lesson of the day—but he didn't get the chance. Mr. Flash was waiting for them at the top of the stairs that led to the Advanced Capability Development Center, barring the way like a bald, bad-tempered bouncer.

"The lesson's taking place outside today," he told them gleefully. "Got some special training for you. There's a war on, you know. **HOP TO IT! HUP TWO, HUP TWO!**"

"What do you think he's got planned?" Billy shivered as they jogged toward the woods with the rest of the class.

"Who knows?" Murph told him. "I can only guarantee that we're not going to like it very much."

"Morning, boys!" called Hilda brightly, catching up with them and dragging Nellie by the hand. "You know what? I'm actually looking forward to CT for once. Our missions are going great, but we could probably use some extra training. **You know, to really**

give the Alliance of Evil a good old **booty-whooping."**

"Whose butt's getting whooped?" Mary asked, smiling, as she too joined the group.

"Magpie and all his minions!" Hilda enthused. "I can feel it. We're going to smash them."

"Nice to have the Super Zeroes together for once," said Billy, looking around at his friends. "You know, it seems like we never get much time with just the five of us these days."

This reminded Murph of his promise to keep his eye on Angel, and he scanned the class for her.

"Who are you looking for?" said Mary, slightly impatiently. "Billy was just saying how nice it was to be all together. You know . . . just the five of us? The Super Zeroes?"

"Oh, yeah," replied Murph absentmindedly. "It's great."

"Well, I for one am actually glad." Mary spoke tartly, but her face told a different story. She looked sad and wistful. Murph was about to explain about his promise to Carl and Flora, but just then he spotted

Angel trotting along not far behind them. She waved and broke into a run to catch up.

"What's up, guys?" she said as she approached. "How's it hanging?"

"People spoke weird in the 1980s," muttered Billy to himself.

"It's hanging very well indeed, thank you, Angel," replied Mary primly. "I hope that you're hanging very excellently too, er, dude." Angel looked at her blankly, and Murph nudged her.

"What?" she hissed at him. "I'm just trying to get on board with the thirty-year-old slang. I thought you of all people would appreciate the effort."

"What's that supposed to mean?" Murph replied, confused. But before he could even begin to unravel what was bothering Mary, they reached the edge of the woods and were forced into single file as the class followed Mr. Flash down a narrow, muddy pathway into the trees.

The path led them to the large pond that stood at the back of Carl's sheds. Murph and the rest of the class lined up along the shore, gazing uneasily at the chilly-looking water—and, even more uneasily, at the unruly pile of barrels, planks, and ropes off to one side.

This was going to be an uncomfortable morning.

"RIGHT," harbinged Colonel Flash. **"NOW AS YOU ALL KNOW, THERE'S A WAR ON!"**

"I think we've got the message," Billy muttered to Murph. "He tells us, like, a couple of times a minute."

"Shut your toad 'ole!" Mr. Flash bellowed at him. "Now listen. I am already a key member of the Heroes' Alliance. With dedication and extremely hard, unpleasant training, some of you may get the chance to join the elite alongside me."

"Some of us are already in the Alliance, Mr. Flash," Mary pointed out.

"SILENCE!" he roared back at her, disturbing a duck that had been hoping for a nice peaceful swim. It paddled away from them with a wounded air.

"The Alliance of Evil is out there," said Mr. Flash portentously. "They will show no mercy. They will attack without warning. But we must be ready to fight."

He puffed his chest out, the medals on his vest catching the sunlight.

"We will fight them on the beaches," began Mr. Flash.

"Seriously?" muttered Mary to herself.

"We will fight them in the shopping centers, and in the vegetable aisles of supermarkets," the teacher continued. "We will fight them in . . . in the trees."

"In the trees?" said someone.

"Yes, in the trees!" Mr. Flash retorted, stung at having his big inspiring speech interrupted like this. "In the trees, in the, er, the go-karting tracks. We will fight them in the superstores, and in the artisan bakeries. And, the point I was trying to get to before I was so rudely interrupted"—he turned and pointed toward the chilly-looking gray water—"we will fight them in the ponds."

"The ponds?" Billy questioned, shivering involuntarily.

"Yers, miladdo," confirmed Mr. Flash. "In the ponds. Which is why I have designed a special training mission this morning to prepare you for aquatical warfare situations. **ALL RIGHT! TIME TO PICK TEAMS!"**

Murph groaned inwardly. The process of picking teams in a gym class is, as we all know, one of the five worst things that ever happen to you at school. They are, in no particular order:

- Dropping your tray in the cafeteria
- Your mom giving you a kiss in front of everyone
- Not realizing it's non-uniform day
- Calling your teacher "Mommy"
- Picking teams for sports

We say "no particular order," but obviously the last one is by far the worst—it's right up there as a contender for single worst thing of all time. It's bad for the people waiting to get picked—the *pickees*, if you like. It's stressful for the picker. It's just not good, is what we're trying to say. And not just because we're bitter that we never got picked first when we were at school. Nope. No siree. Stop snickering.

"ALL RIGHT, COOPER," shouted Colonel Flash. "Since you're the Alliance's current flavor of the decade, you can be our first team captain." Activating his Cape, he whooshed over to Murph, who felt himself grabbed roughly by the shoulders and plucked out of the line. Before he knew it, he was on the shore next to Mr. Flash with the rest of the class facing him.

"Horse girl, you can be the other captain!" Mr. Flash beckoned Hilda over to stand on his other side. "If the Alliance thinks you Super Zeroes are so fiddlin' marvelous, let's see what you're made of, shall we? Right, Cooper, you can pick first. Come on, come on, hurry up. I imagine we can all guess who you're gonna choose. Your little yellow canary friend, is it?"

Murph felt like his tongue had been superglued to the roof of his mouth. Of course he wanted to pick Mary—she was his best friend—but Carl's words were pinging around inside his head: *I know you'll take care of my Angel. We're both counting on you.*

To his horror, he saw that Mary, preempting him, had already left the line of students and started to walk his way. Panic filled his brain like an air-raid siren.

"No!" he blurted out, holding out a hand as if he was trying to stop traffic.

Mary halted mid-stride, halfway between him and the pond. She looked at him quizzically, raising her eyebrows above her glasses in the expression he knew so well.

"Angel," said Murph weakly, wishing heartily that the universe would explode. Mary blushed deeply as some of the class tittered. She was caught in a no-man's-land of humiliation.

"OH HO HO! TROUBLE IN PARADISE!" gloated Colonel Flash in delight.

"No, I didn't mean . . . I mean, I don't *not* want . . ." mumbled Murph weakly, but it was too late. Shooting him a look of total fury, Mary turned on her heel and marched away to the end of the line, wiping her eyes.

"ALL RIGHT THEN, ANGEL, COME AND JOIN YOUR BOYFRIEND!" continued the teacher, beckoning her over.

Angel jogged up to join Murph, holding up her hand for a high five as she did so. He responded so lamely that their hands slapped weakly together like a couple of dead fish.

"Baker, who are you picking?" barked Colonel Flash, still leering at Murph with relish.

"Mary," piped Hilda without hesitation. Mary walked over and hugged her friend, still scarlet with embarrassment.

Murph looked across, trying desperately to mold his face into an expression that combined massive apology with *I'll explain everything later*, but he just ended up looking like he had stepped on a hedgehog in bare feet. Besides, Mary was refusing to meet his eye, glaring out across the pond as if the calm grayish water had personally offended her with its moistness.

Murph picked Billy next; Nellie went to Hilda's team.

It was the first time the Super Zeroes had really been separated, Murph realized with a pang. This pang added to the other massive pang he was already experiencing after being forced to betray his best friend. He had become a walking, talking bag of pangs. A pangolin, if you will. He was pang-tastic. He was pang-icking.

(That doesn't quite work, that last one. But you know what we mean.)

A few minutes later, the teams were complete, with the class divided neatly in two between Murph's and Hilda's.

Among Murph's team was the group of older kids that had caused Murph and his friends so many problems in their first year at The School. For a long time he'd only known these five by the mental nicknames he'd conjured up for them: Gangly Fuzz Face, Pork Belly Pig Breath, Crazy Eyes Jemima, Corned Beef Boy, and Frankenstein's Nephew. But more recently Murph had been forced to rethink his opinion of them. Gangly—or Nathan as we now know he was actually called—had developed a grudging respect for the Super Zeroes and had actually helped them to escape when Magpie had managed to get them declared as Rogue Heroes. And Murph had been reluctantly forced to concede that—just maybe—you shouldn't judge a bully by their cover. Or, at least, you shouldn't judge them purely on an unkind nickname you've made up based on their physical appearance. So while they weren't actually friends, there was certainly a kind of uneasy truce in place.

Also on Murph's team was Elsa, the girl whose Cape was to form ice and snow but was nothing to do with any other character you might have—oh, I dunno—seen in a film or something.

"ALL RIGHT!" thundered Flash. "Now that we've finally finished the emotional helter-skelter of putting the teams together"—he glanced from Murph to Mary "—we can actually start today's mission! I don't know, honestly! It's like one of those terrible romance stories my mom makes me read to her."

"You *what*?" said Billy incredulously. "You read love stories out loud to your mom?"

"BWAAAARGH!" exploded Colonel Flash, realizing in total panic that he'd overshared. *"SHUT YOUR BISCUIT HOLE! DON'T YOU KNOW THERE'S A WAR ON? PUT THAT LIGHT OUT!"*

"What?"

"Shut up!" Mr. Flash collected himself with difficulty.

"I'm about to divulge today's mission. Now, as you know, Heroes are expected to work in all kinds of conditions. Rain, drizzle, downpours, or even wet weather."

"Those are all the same."

"Shut up. Now, over there, on the opposite bank of the pond, is today's objective." He pointed out across the water, and they all peered toward the other side. There, propped up against a bush, was a life-size cloth doll.

"It's Annabel!" exclaimed Hilda excitedly. "She's back!" A few weeks earlier Colonel Flash had given them a similar exercise to rescue a doll from the top of a ladder. It hadn't ended well. In fact it ended as badly as it could have: with Annabel burned to cinders.

"That," retorted Colonel Flash now, "is not Annabel. Annabel is . . . no longer with us." He paused for a moment, out of respect. "That over there," continued their teacher, "is Annabel Too."

"Annabel number two?" Billy wanted to know.

"NO!" snapped the Colonel. *"ANNABEL TOO! T-O-O!* As in, she is also called Annabel. The old doll was Annabel, and this one is called Annabel . . . TOO! Get it? Perfectly simple!"

"Why didn't you just give it a different name?" asked Elsa.

"I have!" Colonel Flash was growing frustrated now. "What have I just told you? She's called Annabel . . ."

"Too, yeah, we know."

"ANYWAY, STOP WASTING TIME LIKE A LOAD OF DITHERING DORMICE! THERE'S A WAR ON! YOUR MISSION TODAY . . ."

"Is to build a raft, cross the pond, and rescue Annabel Too, and the first ones back here win?" suggested Hilda brightly.

Colonel Flash looked at her as if she was a tiny, tiny tadpole swimming around in his lemonade.

"NO!" he fumed. "Your mission . . . is to build a raft, cross the pond, and THEN rescue Annabel Too. And THEN come back over here."

"That's exactly what I just said . . ." Hilda muttered to herself crossly.

"GO!" Colonel Flash had pulled a whistle out of his pocket, and he blew a huge blast that sounded like a giant, angry seagull that had just found out all its fries had been stolen and then shut its toe in a door. Everybody rushed to the water's edge and began to sort through the barrels, ropes, and planks.

Once a couple of minutes had elapsed, Murph looked across and saw that Hilda and Mary had already laid out their barrels in two neat rows and were lashing planks to the top.

"I could use my Cape," Angel said excitedly in Murph's ear as he lugged a heavy barrel down the muddy slope. "You could get Billy to balloon something, then I could copy his power—and magnify it. We could make a mega-raft!"

Murph wasn't sure. Personally, he felt that hands-on things like raft building were probably best achieved without the use of Capes—but on the other hand, he did have specific instructions to make sure Angel was happy and confident at school.

"Um . . . okay. Sure," he said, unable to keep a slight hint of doubt out of his voice.

"Billy," said Angel excitedly, **"Murph wants you to balloon a barrel! Quick!"**

"I'll try," said Billy doubtfully, dropping a coil of rope and coming over. He placed a hand on the plastic, concentrated, and with a **parp!** the barrel inflated.

"My turn," said Angel, clearly excited to try her Cape out again. She grabbed another barrel and held it up. There was a noise like twenty hippopotami all burping at the same time, and it rapidly doubled in size. **"Radical!"** exclaimed Angel. **"Giant Barrelsville, Arizona!"**

"Awesome!" enthused Nathan, beckoning to the rest of the team. "Come on, let's get these lashed together. Nice work, new girl!"

Angel beamed as Murph meekly joined the others roping planks to the top of the two jumbo-size barrels. But their team was still behind. A couple of minutes later, there was a splash and a damp cheer from Hilda's team as they launched their raft and climbed on board. They began paddling toward the opposite bank, lolling low in the water.

Murph's team's raft was rather larger, thanks to the ballooned barrels, so when they hit the water a minute or so later they were a lot more buoyant. Having said that, Angel's barrel at the back was larger than Billy's at the front, so they were tilted forward alarmingly.

Halfway across, it became obvious that all was not well on the good ship *Hilda*. Her raft was getting lower and lower in the water. "She's sinking!" Hilda wailed, as chilly water soaked her socks.

"Looks like they're in trouble over there," said Angel to Murph in a satisfied tone of voice. "Time to slow them down even more. Remember, no points for second place!"

"Check this out," Elsa piped up, shuffling over to the side of the raft. "I've been working on this." She concentrated, holding out a pointing finger. At first, only a chilly mist spilled out of the end—then a stream of sharp shards of ice shot out, forcing the crew on the other raft to duck and scatter, sending it pitching ominously in the water.

"Oooh, cool, ice bullets!" marveled Frankenstein's Nephew.

"Rad, huh?" Angel agreed.

"Um, probably," he replied, baffled.

"Okay, let's see if I can get the hang with that one,"

said Angel, extending an arm and pointing a finger at the other raft. Murph felt a twinge of alarm—in a sense, she had only just discovered this Cape-mirroring, and indeed Cape-magnifying, power. He wasn't sure she should be playing so fast and loose with it. He made a mental note to talk to Carl about this—but the note got lost almost immediately underneath an entire folder marked **"MARY: URGENT."** Even that was pushed from his mental in-box, though, as Angel unleashed her own version of Elsa's icy Capability.

A jet of supercooled air shot from her pointing finger, whizzing across the the pond and freezing the surface of the water as it went. The blast hit the back of Hilda's raft squarely, but instead of damaging it, it propelled it forward rapidly.

"Hang on, everyone!" shouted Hilda as they picked up speed, gliding across the surface of the pond like a perfectly skimmed stone. **"The old girl's been given a boost! Wheeeeeeee!"**

Hilda's raft hit the opposite bank within seconds, and Mary scrambled out and plucked Annabel Too from the undergrowth.

"Whoo-ah!" Angel exulted. **"Ice blast!**
Did you guys see that?"

"We saw the other team winning," Nathan replied grumpily. "Come on, Team Captain, what's the plan?"

Murph looked at him blankly. He just wanted this day to end so he could go home, crawl into bed, and hide underneath his comforter until several years had passed. The more he thought about the way he'd just humiliated Mary in front of the whole class, the more his stomach curled up like a contortionist shrimp.

"Oh, forget it!" snapped Nathan, his wispy mustache fluttering in contempt. "I'm taking control of this."

"Mutiny!" Billy scolded, but nobody heard him except Murph—and he only managed a weak, watery smile.

"All right!" Nathan was telling the rest of the crew. "We've got to stop them from getting Alison back to shore!"

"Annabel Too," someone corrected him.

"Whatever!" The other raft had now turned around, and Hilda's team was beginning to paddle back across the pond. "I reckon if I make a force field in the water, and spin it," Nathan continued, "I can slow them down a bit." He concentrated, and the water in the center of the pond began to turn sluggishly in a circle.

"Faster! It's working!" urged Crazy Eyes Jemima.

"I got this," Angel told the rest of the team reassuringly. And before anyone had time to stop her, she had activated her own more-powerful version of Nathan's force-field Cape.

"Gah! Whirlpool!" screamed Hilda from the other raft. And she was right. Angel's magnified force field had created a very scary-looking maelstrom of water. "Paddle around it!" shouted Hilda desperately.

Her team tried their best, but it was hopeless. Both rafts were sucked toward the swirling waters. Angel's whoop of excitement turned into a whimper of fear, which sounded like this: **"Whooooooooo . . . Whaaaaaargh."** There was a sound like two rafts crashing into each other as the two rafts crashed into each other. *Crack!* Barrels boinged, planks plonked, and ropes ripped.

Watching from the bank in total fury, Colonel Flash hopped from foot to foot. "What in the name of Blackbeard's . . . beard do you bunch of nautical ninnies think you're playing at?" he roared, but was silenced when the storm surge hit the bank and drenched him.

Gradually the whirlpool slowed and stopped, leaving a selection of raft components, most of which had children clinging to them, bobbing around on the surface.

Everyone splashed their way to the shore and dragged themselves out through the muddy bank. Colonel Flash glared at the collection of sopping mud creatures ranged in front of him. **"YOU LOAD OF USELESS SEA CUCUMBERS! WHERE'S ANNABEL TOO?"**

Meekly Hilda stepped forward, holding up a sodden, shapeless object with two button eyes. It was

Annabel's head. She was gripping it by the hair at arm's length, unintentionally looking like a gruesome medieval doll executioner.

"Is that . . ." Colonel Flash was such a deep, furious red color he looked like he might actually catch fire.

"IS THAT . . . ANNABEL TOO'S HEAD?"

Hilda nodded.

"Stop holding it up by the hair!"

Hilda dropped the head to the ground, where it landed with a soggy, coconut-cream-pie splat.

"I spent hours sewing her . . ." Colonel Flash seemed to be having trouble getting his words out. "Go and get yourselves dried off . . ."

"Are you *crying*?" asked Jemima.

"NO, IT'S POND WATER. HOW DARE YOU," babbled Colonel Flash, picking up Annabel Too's head and cradling it.

He turned away from them and stalked off through the trees, sniffing intermittently.

Gradually the class headed for the changing rooms to get dry clothes on. Murph was desperate to talk to Mary to try to explain why he'd picked Angel first, but as soon as Colonel Flash had said, "Go and get yourselves dried off," she had grabbed Hilda by the hand and rushed away up the slope toward The School. Billy and Nellie, too, had wandered off, Nellie shooting Murph a single, disappointed glance from behind her straggly wet hair.

"Well, that didn't quite go to plan." Angel grinned at him. **"Fun, though, wasn't it?"**

Murph grunted sourly. He couldn't tell Angel he'd picked her for his team first only because he'd promised her dad. And he couldn't puncture her good mood by telling her it was her overenthusiastic use of her Cape that had lost them the race. Plus, he couldn't even begin to explain to himself why Mary had been so obviously upset and furious.

He felt like he was drowning in misery, and he looked and smelled like he'd just nearly drowned in a pond. Angel took his tragic expression for frustration that he hadn't won and tried to cheer him up.

"Look, don't stress about all that nonsense," she told him. "There's a limit to what you can do without a Cape. It's not like you can be expected to suddenly take control of a whole team of Heroes!"

Murph looked up.

"Oh . . . no! Sorry." She looked embarrassed. "I didn't mean it like that. I know you're in the Alliance and all that. Great work on the plane and everything. I just meant . . . you know . . ."

"No, no, I know what you mean," Murph told her. And for a split second the thought came to him: What *would* it be like to have a Cape like hers? A solid, identifiable ability that everyone could rely on? He sighed, wringing pond water out of his sleeve.

Angel smiled at him awkwardly. "Keep your chin up, yeah?" She glanced through the trees toward the janitor's huts. "Look, there's my dad! I'm gonna say hi. Want to come?"

Together they trailed damply along the path and up to the balcony, where Carl was sitting in his usual deck chair. "Looks like you're having an interesting day," he told them, looking at their soaked clothes and matted hair.

"Yeah, it was totally fun!" Angel told him. "I'm just gonna change. See you in a sec." She disappeared through the wooden door.

"Thanks, Captain, I knew I could rely on you," Carl told Murph, giving him a friendly tip of his checked cap. Murph responded with a watery smile and a meek wave. He let out a sigh, turning away from his friend and wandering back down the stairs into the wood.

He walked toward the changing rooms, kicking twigs moodily as he went. Somehow, alarmingly, this one single class seemed to have cracked the rock-solid friendship of the Super Zeroes in half like a fossil-fancier hammer.

8

Titan Thirteen

As Murph Cooper's wet and muddy sneakers were clomping their moody way back across the playing fields toward The School, two very different and much cleaner shoes were making a journey of their own, many miles away.

The shoes were black and highly polished. So highly polished, in fact, that they reflected the world back upon itself. A darker version of the world was mirrored in those shoes, though. A world with the color and life bled out of it.

The shoes belonged to Nicholas Knox, and they were clanging arrogantly on a metal floor as they carried him along the side of a large control panel studded with screens, dials, and switches. Knox tweaked the sleeves of his expensive suit, running his hand over a bank of small levers and flicking one of them down with a manicured finger. A nearby screen was displaying a readout of numbers, and he smiled to himself in satisfaction as he checked it.

Sunshine streamed into the room through an enormous oval window in the ceiling. The glass was dusty and cracked in places, giving the light a strange texture—almost as though the huge space was underwater. The tops of two gigantic concrete chimneys could be seen through the window.

"All in order, Mr. Knox?" The croaky voice echoed around the cavernous space. "Is the Shadow Machine ready?"

Knox answered without turning around. "Yes, indeed. My final checks are now complete." He had not heard Magpie approaching but suddenly a spindly, long-fingered hand landed on his shoulder. He kept calm, flicking the lever back into place and checking the digits on the screen one last time. Only then did he turn to survey his handiwork.

"Excellent news." Magpie walked away from him again, toward the huge metal structure in the middle of the room. The Shadow Machine looked like a pyramid with its top half sliced off. It was constructed of metal girders and mesh, with a bizarre collection of huge cogs, wheels, and gears visible inside. It almost filled the central area of the massive room. Iron staircases led up the middle of each of the four sides, and Magpie now began to climb one of these.

"Magpie and Nicholas Knox! However did these two villains end up working together?" we hear you ask. Well, we can't actually *hear* you, that would be creepy. But we imagine you're asking that question. In fact one of you might even have written it down and mailed it to us. Hang on, there's the doorbell. Oh, would you believe it? It's the mail carrier. He's brought us this brief letter. Let's read it, shall we?

Dear Authors of the Bestselling Kid Normal Series,
RE: Magpie and Nicholas Knox.
However did these two villains end up working together?
Sincerely yours,
A. Reader.

What an excellent question. And just because you took the time to write in, we'll tell you. Here goes. . .

Nicholas Knox, as we've said before, was an ambitious man. And not in the good way. He wasn't ambitious, for instance—just to pluck an example out of the air—to Give All Puppies the Best Saturday Morning Ever. That would be an awesome ambition. He wasn't ambitious—to think of another totally random example— to Use His Huge Scientific Expertise to Clone a Unicorn Like in *Jurassic Park* Only with Rainbows. No. In fact, unbelievable as it may sound, that idea hadn't even crossed his mind. Nicholas Knox was ambitious in a far less cool and far more dangerous way. He was ambitious, purely and simply, to Make Himself More Successful. The emptiest and, ultimately, the least satisfying of all ambitions. His goal was for Team Knox to win—and he was the only member of that team. Other people might be useful as cheerleaders, as advisers, as playthings. But at the end of the game, he wanted to be the only person standing on the field, with no friends, holding up a big, useless silver cup.

Ever since discovering the secret world of Heroes,

Knox had been racking his brains to work out how it could ultimately benefit him. And then, out of the blue, Magpie had sought him out some weeks ago. Suddenly, Knox was face-to-face with a man who claimed to be the most powerful enemy the Heroes had ever gone up against. And he was asking Knox for help! It felt like his birthday (and completely incidentally, it actually was, only nobody had given him any presents because selfish people end up alone—**LIFE LESSON**).

Anyway. . . Magpie told Nicholas Knox about his plan to build a machine. "A machine such as the world has never seen," he had explained. "Because even with the myriad of different powers at my disposal, I am not able to penetrate the secrets of the human mind. But I have heard tales of your mind-control technology. And I believe that by combining my own tele-tech with your scientific expertise, we can create something truly astonishing."

Knox had barely paused to think. In villain terms, this was a total no-brainer. Here was the most powerful Rogue of them all—a man who could destroy him a thousand different ways—actually offering to collaborate with him. The two men, as men will so often do, agreed to work together, with each secretly thinking of the other as a mere pawn in their own larger game. And so Magpie had brought Nicholas Knox to his secret headquarters. A base, he revealed, that the Heroes' Alliance had never discovered even during his long years of imprisonment. He had brought him to Titan Thirteen.

The Titan Thirteen power plant had been state-of-the-art once, when it was first built. But when Knox had arrived it had seemed utterly derelict. Magpie had explained to him that this was all part of the cover—that decades ago he had ensured that the plant had been declared unsafe and abandoned. While he languished in prison, it had lain dormant for years, moldering and crumbling away on an isolated patch of land hidden behind craggy hills. Warning signs and barbed wire had kept out curious people, ensuring the site remained completely deserted, save for the cawing birds that still nested on the crumbling window ledges.

But, Knox quickly discovered, Titan Thirteen had a secret. It may have appeared derelict, but Magpie had ensured that it was still operational. Still connected to the power grid. Waiting for its master to return. It was here, in the cellars beneath the abandoned buildings, that he had organized the Alliance of Evil. It was here that he had summoned the escaped Rogues of Shivering Sands to goad them into war. And it was here that he planned to begin work on his ultimate revenge.

Nicholas Knox had been assigned what had once been the main control room of Titan Thirteen. The original architect had had grand ideas, describing this as a "Palace of Power" and designing the cavernous room accordingly. Pillars of cast iron marched down each wall. The doors were huge and ornate. And above Knox's head, that huge oval window filtered the sunbeams into a strange, ethereal light.

And here, over the past several weeks, the two men had been working tirelessly. Knox had been astonished at the way Magpie's Capabilities were able to bring his ideas to life. The man in black was quite literally able to communicate with electronic circuitry, forging it into the most complicated systems with a casual flick of his hand. With his other powers he was able to twist and

shape metal, lifting and placing it to Knox's specifications as the Shadow Machine took shape. And now, finally, it was ready.

While you were reading that last page, Magpie was climbing the metal staircase. And just at this point, as you're reading this exact sentence here, he reached the flattened top of the pyramid—an area around the size of a tennis court. Knox, still standing beside his control panels, could see the black shape moving restlessly around, rubbing its hands together. The top of the Shadow Machine was bare, except for two plinths at either end. Each was topped with a clear glass orb—lifeless and still for the moment.

"Prepared for power-up," Knox called, and saw the distant figure raise a hand in affirmation. Knox flicked a whole bank of switches down with his palm. There was a deep hum, almost inaudible, and a slight vibration in the floor. The dials on the control panels lit up and the needles began to twitch and flick.

For miles and miles around, people looked up in confusion as the lights in their houses dimmed. Computers crashed as their power supply failed, and supermarket self-checkouts failed to work efficiently—although to be fair, that last one was nothing to do with the machine draining their power supply; it was just because they're badly designed.

A purple light began to flicker and glow within the twin orbs on the top of the Shadow Machine. It pulsed and spun around inside the glass like a living thing, as if some kind of ghost was trapped inside. Knox narrowed his eyes in satisfaction. The machine was channeling Magpie's brain waves. Keeping one wary eye on the control panel, he looked around at the eerie purple glow that was now filling the room. He could see that Magpie had moved to stand behind one of the twin orbs. "Bring in the guinea pig!" he was shouting.

Knox licked his lips, shoulders tense with excitement as the huge metal double doors at one end of the room clanked into action. *The time has come. We're about to discover whether this machine can really work.* Even now, Knox's mind reeled a little with the audacity of what this giant metal pyramid was designed to do. He wondered which of his hench-persons Magpie had selected to be the first to test it. But he was slightly startled to see who actually did walk through the doors. It was a plump little man with a tuft of red hair that stuck straight out of his head and extremely large black eyes. He was holding an entire iceberg lettuce in one hand, and eating it much like you would an apple.

"Eeeeeeee," squeaked the man. **"You wanted to seee meee?"** He took another crunching bite of lettuce.

Knox looked up at Magpie curiously.

"This," Magpie explained from the top of the pyramid, "is Guinea Pig. Former inmate of Shivering Sands, imprisoned for serial salad theft. He will be used today as a way of testing out the machine . . ."

"As . . . a guinea pig, in fact?" clarified Knox.

"Exactly. One of the most terrifying Rogues in our whole Alliance," Magpie lied. "Let us begin."

"Lettuce?" squealed Guinea Pig excitedly.

"Come, my friend. You and I are about to make history," announced Magpie. **"Join me!"** Guinea Pig scuttled up the staircase joyously, muttering to himself about lettuces. Magpie gestured for Guinea Pig to take up a position opposite him on the platform, behind the second glowing orb.

Knox squinted upward at the two figures atop the pyramid, beneath the huge dusty window.

"This is the Shadow Machine," Magpie was now announcing grandly, "the most incredible piece of technology this planet will ever see. A machine that could only have been conceived by the most brilliant brain in history."

Knox curled his lip slightly. It had been *his* engineering brilliance that had made the Shadow Machine a reality. It's always the same with villains. To start with it's all "Let's work together," and then when the evil plans actually come to fruition it's suddenly "Oh look, my evil plan has succeeded, aren't I brilliant?" And you're supposed to feel privileged just to have been part of the plan at all.

"You should feel very privileged to be part of this plan," Magpie told Guinea Pig. "You are about to make history. The first to ever step inside my mind. For that is the power of the Shadow Machine. It will allow our two minds to join . . . and you will be able to choose one of my many powers and take it for your own."

Guinea Pig gave an enthusiastic squeak: **"Eeeee!"**

"Yes, you're right to be excited. Shall we?"

Magpie placed his hands on the orb in front of him and nodded for Guinea Pig to do the same. Knox, looking on, felt a thrill of excitement. This was the moment when he would discover whether his technology worked.

The instant Guinea Pig placed his own pudgy, hairy hands on the orb in front of him, the Shadow Machine clanked into life. The gears and wheels underneath began to spin, and the dancing lights inside the orb swirled faster and faster. The rest of the room seemed to grow darker as a cube of bright light formed around the platform. It was piercingly bright, changing the two figures on top into stark silhouettes. A swirling mist seemed to fill the cube, and as Knox watched, faint shadows spread out from Magpie—thin, indistinct specters he thought he could see through the white light. But it was too bright to look at them for long.

"Can you see them, my piggy friend?" Magpie's voice rang out. "Move among them. You can roam freely. That's right. . . keep moving. You are now in the very midst of my powers . . ."

Knox's mind was alight with curiosity. He knew that the machine had given Guinea Pig access to Magpie's mind, and his powers. But from his vantage point at the control panel, all he could see was two motionless figures, frozen in place with their hands glued to the orbs. His long fingers twitched with curiosity to discover what it was like to actually enter the Shadow Machine.

"**Butterflies?**" he heard Guinea Pig say suddenly, in a high-pitched, hesitant voice.

"Excellent choice. Yes, very pretty," he heard Magpie

say patronizingly. "Just step into the shadow . . . and it shall be yours."

After a moment, the humming and clanking from the depths of the Shadow Machine increased in pitch and volume. The dials on Knox's control panel began to twitch and spin and he realized that Guinea Pig had indeed made his choice. The cube of white light became more and more intense until it was impossible to look at it directly.

And then, suddenly, the light was gone. The gears inside the great machine slowed and stopped. The two figures on top lifted their hands from the orbs as the lights inside the glass spheres flickered and went out.

Magpie, who looked pale and ill, was panting. Guinea Pig, on the other hand, seemed dazed. His huge dark eyes were bright with excitement as he lifted his hands up in front of him. He let out a squeal of excitement as a stream of bright purple butterflies burst from his palm, firing upward to dance around in the beams of sunlight streaming through the dusty window in the ceiling.

Knox was awestruck. His machine had worked. He had no idea what Magpie or Guinea Pig had just experienced, but one thing was undeniable: a superpower had been transferred from one to the other. He trembled with excitement at what this discovery might mean. **"It works!"** he called up to the platform.

"It works," confirmed Magpie calmly, before turning to Guinea Pig. "I'm glad you're enjoying my butterfly power, friend. I'm almost tempted to let you keep it. But that's not really how I operate."

Crackling jets of purple forked lightning shot out of his hands and surrounded Guinea Pig—who dropped to his knees as his butterflies exploded like tiny puffs of smoke. He squeaked in anguish, struggled to his feet and fled down the stairs and out of the room, only stopping briefly to pick up his half-eaten lettuce.

Knox watched him go, then turned back to see Magpie stalking down the metal stairs.

"Experiment complete, Knox", said the man in black. "And I would call that an unmitigated success, wouldn't you? Reset the chamber. Prepare it for another transfer. The next person to step into this machine will be Kid Normal. The darling of the Heroes' Alliance." His lip curled savagely.

Nicholas Knox was dumbfounded. He had assumed that Magpie wanted this machine to create an army of supervillains. He couldn't for the life of him think what purpose could possibly be served by giving powers to one of his enemies. "Heroes' Alliance?" he faltered. **"You want to give a power to . . . a Hero?"**

"Ah, Mr. Knox," purred Magpie, walking over and regarding him coldly. "You still have a lot to learn. You are ambitious, clinical, ruthless . . . all excellent qualities. You show real potential. But you fail to appreciate what it takes to really crush the human spirit."

"I don't understand," Knox admitted. "I don't see why you would want to give one of your enemies such a reward. After all, you're fighting a war against them!"

And now Magpie laughed. It was a sharp, cracking sound that filled the enormous echoing room with a sound like beaks pecking stones. "War?" he cackled. "War? My dear Knox, this whole war is nothing but a smoke screen. A distraction to keep the Heroes busy while I get on with my real work. And as for a reward . . . you think this is about giving the boy who ruined my plans a *reward*?"

Magpie turned and walked toward the double doors. "This isn't about *reward*, Knox."

A soft rain of purple butterfly wings was falling between them as he stalked away.

"It's about *revenge*."

9

Parents' Morning

Murph did his best to right the Super Zeroes' capsized friendship after the raft race fiasco, but it was far from smooth sailing.

The next time he managed to talk to all his friends together was at lunchtime the next day. Mary, Billy, Hilda, and Nellie were sitting together in the cafeteria when he came in, and he made a beeline for the empty chair next to Mary. She greeted him with that kind of distant politeness that means "I am angry with you but I am far too angry to tell you that I'm angry with you so I'm going to be polite to you and nothing more."

"Look," said Murph without preamble. "About yesterday's CT class . . ."

"Yeah," Billy broke in, "what *about* yesterday's CT class? **I found a frog in my pocket later on. A frog!**"

"I don't think Murph wants to hear about your pocket frog," said Mary tartly. "I think he wants to tell us why he picked—"

"Angel!" interrupted Hilda. **"Angel! Over here!"**

Angel was holding a tray of food and spinning around in the famous lunchtime looking-for-someone-to-sit-with dance. She spotted Hilda waving and jogged over, smiling. "What's up! You all okay?" she said as she sat down. "I just got out of geography. Who knew there was a tunnel to France? Under the sea! That's crazy!"

Murph grinned despite himself. He had come to realize that, for all her breezy nature, almost everything about daily life was a startling culture shock for Angel. Every aspect of The School was strange and rare, from the cars on the street outside to the pens in people's pockets. Even lunch could be a startling experience— and today's was no exception. School chef Bill Burton had served up one of his specialties: spicy Moroccan couscous.

"What in the name of Starsky and Hutch is this supposed to be?"

she asked, holding up a steaming forkful. "It's, like, crumbs? Or tiny, tiny little potatoes with green things on them? Is this what boiled potatoes look like to a giant?"

"This isn't what you used to eat in the 1980s, then?" asked Mary a little wearily.

"No way!" exclaimed Angel, taking a bite. **"This is, like, food from the future! It's tubular!"**

"So, um, Angel," said Hilda. "I was going to ask you about the raft race yesterday . . ."

"Oh, yeah, sorry about that." Angel blushed. "Don't know the strength of my own Cape yet, really. Didn't mean to sink you."

"No, no, it's fine," soothed Hilda. "I was just wondering . . . what is your Cape, exactly? I've never seen anything like that."

Murph felt a lurch of guilt that he still hadn't told his friends about the story he'd heard in Carl's workshop. "She can copy other people's Capes after they use them, but do them better. Kind of magnify them!" he explained to Hilda.

"Oh, you knew all about it already, did you?" said

Mary crossly. "I might have known." She snatched up her tray and abruptly left the table.

"What's grinding her engine?" Angel asked, looking concerned.

"Don't worry, it's nothing you did," Murph reassured her.

"What a cool Cape," Hilda was saying. "I've never heard of anyone who could do that!"

"Me neither," Angel said nonchalantly, taking another mouthful of couscous from the future.

It's amazing how quickly a week can roll by when you're in charge of a team of superheroes who are all feeling semi-awkward around you, and you're in the middle of a war against a huge gang of escaped villains who have sworn to destroy you. Trust us, it really eats into your day. Before Murph really knew what was happening, he was waking up the following Thursday and remembering, with a cold splash of foreboding, that today was the day he had to take his mom to his secret super-school for a completely fake Parents' Night, first thing in the morning.

"I'm so excited!" Murph's mom enthused as they walked through town in the cold dawn light. "I've heard so much about what goes on at your school. Well—" she thought for a moment—"I've heard bits and pieces about it. But it'll be great to finally see it for myself!"

Murph was sunk in thought and only managed a weak bleat in response. He was replaying the previous week to himself, and he wasn't enjoying the show. Mentally he tallied it all up:

Heroes' Alliance missions undertaken	**3**
Heroes' Alliance missions Angel has tagged along on even though that probably isn't strictly allowed	**3**
Rogues recaptured	**1**
Times I have displayed great leadership	**0**
Times I have not displayed great leadership because the atmosphere in our team of Heroes is really weird all of a sudden and it's basically my fault	**3**
Times Angel has knocked out the power to an entire village by copying Nellie's Cape and getting overexcited	**1**
Conversations with Mary that started off awkwardly but ended up really well after I explained everything to her honestly	**0**
Conversations with Mary that started off awkwardly and also ended awkwardly because I failed to explain everything to her honestly	**9**

As the credits rolled on his mental movie, he made a decision. It couldn't go on like this. But first he had to get through this ridiculous fake Parents' Night Morning. He steeled himself as he approached the gates, nodding to the single Cleaner on duty behind the sandbags.

"What's all this?" his mom was saying.

"Escaped giraffe, madam, nothing to worry about. We have the situation totally under control," the Cleaner reassured her.

"Escaped *what?*"

"Ah, good morning, Ms. Cooper," interrupted the booming voice of Mr. Souperman. He was approaching across the school's front yard, extending a large chiseled hand. (Yes, you can get chiseled hands, we checked. And anyway, we can do what we like—we make this stuff up.) "Or may I perhaps call you . . ." At this point the principal realized that he didn't actually know Murph's mom's first name. "May I perhaps call you . . . *Ms.* Cooper?" he tried, emphasizing the "Ms." in a frankly ludicrous fashion.

"Katie will do, actually," said Murph's mom, taking

his hand and giving it a firm shake. "That man said something about an escaped—"

"Katie! Well, well, well," enthused Mr. Souperman, completely ignoring her. **"What a lovely name. Welcome, Katie, to our school. Our wonderful, perfectly normal school."**

Murph gave the principal a glare, making his eyes go so wide that they looked like they might actually pop out and smack Mr. Souperman in the face.

It had been bad enough explaining to his mom that Parents' Night would take place before school in the morning. And now, thanks to Mr. Souperman's total inability to operate under any kind of social pressure, the weirdness gauge was creeping up by the second.

"Good morning, Murph," the principal greeted him. **"My, what big eyes you have."**

Now he's turning into a fairy-tale wolf, thought Murph to himself. To distract from the strained atmosphere, he grabbed his mom's hand and started to pull her through the gates with a cheery "Shall we have a look around?"

"Yes, yes," said Mr. Souperman, following them. "Allow me to give you a tour of our perfectly standard school facilities, um, Ms. Katie."

"No, it's fine," insisted Murph. "I'll do it."

"Nay, nay," countered the principal, wagging a roguish finger and sounding increasingly unhinged, "I must be allowed to escort your, ah, charming Cooper. That is to say, Ms. Mother." He held out an elbow and waggled his eyebrows. Murph's mom grabbed on to his arm, needing both hands to do so, and was practically lifted off her feet as he swept off into the school grounds.

"Ordinary coatrooms over here—just as you would find in any normal school," he told her, waving his free arm as they went.

Murph cringed. The principal was totally overdoing the whole "ordinary school" bit, but he couldn't think of any way to get the message across.

"Conventional playing fields out the back there," Mr. Souperman continued. "Running track, um, hurdles. Couple of sandpits. All very, very ordinary . . ."

"No, it's very nice," encouraged Katie, thinking the principal was being a little too modest about the school facilities. "It's all lovely—really very, very special."

Mr. Souperman stopped short. **"Special?"** he said, a little sharply. **"No it isn't."**

"It is, really," said Murph's mom kindly. "Murph always tells me how special this place is."

"Does he?" asked the principal suspiciously, turning to Murph. "Do you?"

"Yes, like every boy thinks his school and his friends are special," said Murph. "It's a *perfectly normal* thing to say."

"Good! Excellent," said the principal. "I

wouldn't want the wonderful Katie Mother thinking it's some kind of weird school. **Like a school for superheroes or something. A ha-ha-ha, ha ha ha ha!!"** It's safe to say that Mr. Souperman was panicking.

"Let's go inside, shall we, Mr. Souperman?" said Murph, a little desperately. "And see if some *other families* are here at, um, Parents' Morning?"

"Ah yes, the other families! Super! No, not super, excellent! Just excellently normal," blubbered Mr. Souperman, sweating freely from his forehead, nose, and, indeed, eyelashes. His face looked like a glazed doughnut.

Murph rolled his eyes. This really shouldn't be that complicated.

"Come on," he prompted, "let's move on." He grabbed his mom's other arm, so that it now looked like she was being marched through the back doors of The School and down the corridor toward the main hall.

"Normal classroom there," said Mr. Souperman, pointing to their left. "That's where Spanish is learned,

204

I believe. And over here"—he hesitated before opening another door and peering gingerly through—"yes, the math classroom. You can see some math on the wall there."

Murph's mom walked into what was, admittedly, one of The School's more normal-looking classrooms. Their math teacher, Mr. Gunthorpe, was famously no-nonsense, and nobody dared activate their Cape in his classes.

"And how is Murph performing at math?" asked Katie.

"Oh, splendidly!" said Mr. Souperman. "He's almost completed it, I believe. Haven't you, young man?" Murph looked at him in blank incomprehension. "Almost completed all the math?" pressed the principal.

Murph laughed weakly and said, "Just a bit of a math in-joke there, Mom. But yeah, I'm doing okay."

His mom smiled at him a little doubtfully as Mr. Souperman led them back out into the hallway.

"Classroom, classroom . . ." he ticked off as he went. "Nothing behind this door at all," he added as they passed the nondescript gray door that led to the

ACDC. "And look, another family enjoying their Parents' Morning!" he declared, as Carl, Flora, and Angel came around the corner.

"Nothing behind that door? What do you mean?" asked Katie.

"Hah! Ha-ha-haa!" panicked Mr. Souperman. "It is . . . a surprise."

"NO IT ISN'T," broke in Murph. "That's not the right word."

"Right word for what?" asked Flora, coming up to them.

"For what's behind that door," said Murph between gritted teeth.

"Just a cupboard, isn't it?" said Flora, winking at him slightly.

Murph sighed with relief. At last, someone with at least basic acting ability.

"Cupboard! That's it, of course," said Mr. Souperman. "Not 'surprise'—'cupboard.' It's a surprise cupboard. Always a surprise to me, because I always forget it's there. Ha ha-ha!"

"Flora Walden, pleased to meet you," said Flora, holding out her hand for Murph's mom to shake.

"This is my husband, Carl, and this is our dau— our *grand*daughter, Angel."

"Hello," said Katie, shaking hands all around. "Do you and Angel know each other, Murph?"

Murph considered his answer to this question. *"Yes, I rescued her from a secret laboratory behind a waterfall where she'd been frozen in time for thirty years by the world's most feared supervillain, and she's been causing me to question my whole identity ever since"* was obviously out, so he settled for "Yeah, we have English together. Hey, Angel".

"Hi," said Angel, looking like she was holding in a smile.

Suddenly something alarming happened. The door of the "cupboard" burst open and Colonel Flash emerged, looking around at them all in surprise as they stared at him, dumbstruck. "What are you all here for?" he demanded.

"What are you doing in the cupboard?" asked Murph's mom faintly.

"CUPBOARD?" sputtered Colonel Flash. **"WHAT DO YOU MEAN,**

CUPBOARD? I'M JUST CHECKING UP ON THE ACDC."

"He's an electrician!" said Angel suddenly. Colonel Flash looked at her furiously, but she silenced him with a meaningful look. "He's an electrician," she repeated, "and he's checking the AC—the air-conditioning—and the DC—the, um, direct current. In the cupboard. Isn't that right, Electrician Bob?"

"ELECTRICIAN BOB?" scoffed Colonel Flash.

"We call him that," explained Angel, "because his name's Bob. And he's . . ."

"AN ELECTRICIAN,"

finished everyone in unison.

"Great Parents' Morning, isn't it?" added Angel.

"It's been a wonderful Parents' Night Morning," said Mr. Souperman gratefully. "Hope you enjoyed it, Mother Cooper."

"That's it?" said Katie.

"What do you mean?"

"Well, aren't we going to meet any of his teachers? Find out how he's doing?"

"I told you, he's doing excellently! Math is almost complete . . ."

"Stop saying that," muttered Murph desperately.

"Everything else . . . ticking along. Grades are, you know . . . there. You've seen some classrooms. He has a friend"—Mr. Souperman indicated Angel—"and a . . . a bag. Shoes. And hair. His hair looks good. All excellent progress."

"But what about—"

"Rest assured," Mr. Souperman told her, enclosing her entire shoulder in one hand and steering her toward the front doors, "we'll call you if there's a problem. **Murph is in excellent hands here, and we're very proud to have him at our ordinary school."**

"He's right, you know," said Flora, looking at Murph with a smile that was as warm and welcome as a freshly baked cupcake. "We're all very proud of him. He's a very special young man."

"He certainly is," added Carl, with one arm around Angel's shoulders.

Katie looked a little baffled, but allowed herself to be led back to the front doors. **"Parents' Morning accomplished. Good day to you, Katie Mother!"** boomed Mr. Souperman, ushering her out as quickly as possible.

"See you at home later, then, Mom!" said Murph.

His mom looked at him in a worryingly direct way and took him to one side. "Yes, see you at home," she told him. "When I think we'll sit down and have a nice long chat about school, shall we? Because that was one of the weirdest things that has ever happened. See you later." Grim-faced, she turned on her heel and marched out of the school gates.

Murph went back through the main doors, his mind whirring and clanking like a late-eighteenth-century loom as he tried to work out how on earth he was going to smooth this over with his mom later. She was going to have a lot of very, very difficult-to-answer questions for him. He could feel them emerging over the horizon like approaching bison.

"YOU'RE ALL BONKERS, YOU PEOPLE,' Colonel Flash was saying to the Waldens

and Mr. Souperman in the hallway. "You look at me like I'm the weird one. Heck, I don't know . . ." He wandered away, shaking his head and tutting. **"ELECTRICIAN BOB? HA! NEVER HEARD SUCH A LOAD OF OLD SOCKS IN MY LIFE."**

10

The Adventure of the Empty House

The sky was already darkening as Murph headed home from school, a hidden sunset giving the packed clouds an unwholesome brownish glow. He'd been dreading this moment all day. It had driven all thoughts of smoothing things over with the rest of the Super Zeroes right out of his mind.

Murph puffed out his cheeks in frustration, resolving to talk to them tomorrow. He'd just explain that he'd been told to look after Angel, that he'd promised to.

That's what I should have done from the beginning, he thought. *I don't know why I didn't just come right out and say it.* Mary, Hilda, Billy, and Nellie were his best friends in the whole world. He could tell them anything. He could tell them things he couldn't even tell his mom.

His stomach fizzed at the thought of Mom. How on earth was he going to explain away that bizarre Parents' Morning? Was he going to have to come clean about The School, and swear her to secrecy? But then what would happen if she tried to contact the police about it, or the town council? The Cleaners would get involved, he supposed. They ruthlessly hushed up any Hero activity. Plus, there was a war going on. He couldn't put her in danger. No. Best that his mom knew nothing. He'd just have to bluster his way out of this as best he could.

But as Murph Cooper approached his front gate he realized that something else was very, very wrong at home. At first he couldn't quite work out what it was, or understand why his body was filled with such a sickening, crushing sense of doom. And then it clicked.

The house was in darkness.

He knew his mom wasn't working that day—in fact he'd been expecting her to be waiting at the front door wearing that "Let's-have-a-chat-shall-we-young-man" expression that meant he was in deep trouble.

But there was no mom. No expression. And, even more worryingly, no front door.

Murph dashed up the front path, sweat breaking out down his back.

The entire door was missing—splintered wood sticking out palely where the hinges had been ripped off. He found it lying near the old well, its blue paint battered and chipped.

"Mom? Hello?" called Murph tentatively, knowing there would be no reply.

He stepped into the hall and looked around. Immediately he knew that there'd been some kind of struggle. The umbrella stand had been knocked over, and in the kitchen at the back of the house, broken glass glittered in the twilight.

"Andy?" called Murph. His voice echoed dully back at him from the unspeaking walls.

Growing up, Murph had always been told that you should call the police in a situation like this. But they could be of no help here. He knew in his bones that this was something to do with the Alliance of Evil. *And anyway*, he realized, with a shock of helplessness, *I'm a member of the Heroes' Alliance.* These days, if the police encountered a crime they couldn't explain or solve, there was every chance that they might call him.

As he stood there, paralyzed with indecision, a face swam into his mind. The face of the first person he could always turn to.

It was Mary's face, with her round glasses and her quizzical, challenging expression. Another bout of queasiness hit him like a breaking wave as he thought about how rocky their friendship had been lately. But despite everything that had happened between them in the past couple of weeks, he knew in that moment, with unshakeable clarity, that none of it mattered. This was an emergency. Mary would always help, and together they'd work out what to do. Everything else was just trivial.

But before he could act, before he could lift his HALO unit or turn back through the doorway, a voice stopped him.

"Murph . . ."

It was faint, and yet it carried eerily through the deserted house. It made Murph's entire skin pucker into goose bumps. Because he knew exactly whose voice it was. And at the sound of that voice, all the most horrifying thoughts he'd been keeping caged up at the back of his brain broke free and engulfed him like dark, flapping birds.

It was the voice of Magpie.

"Murph."

He followed the voice up the creaking staircase. Past Andy's dark room and up the second flight of stairs to his own attic bedroom.

Here the voice was clearer, its mocking tone urging him onward.

"Murph."

As he watched the thin, early moon spill pale light across his bedroom floor, Murph realized with a shock where the voice was coming from. He dropped to his knees and began rummaging under the bed, pulling out a battered cardboard box filled with junk. Old toys, sheets of paper, and notebooks were scattered inside. But from underneath them came a strange purplish glow.

Murph plunged his hand down the side, and after a moment he produced a sleek black handset just like a smartphone. This was his original HALO unit, the one he'd been presented with by Miss Flint on the day he'd first joined the Alliance. After the system had been hacked by Magpie and the Heroes had abandoned the handsets altogether, Murph had chucked it in the box so his mom didn't ask any awkward questions. But now the screen was active once again.

Magpie was using the abandoned HALO network to broadcast directly to him.

"Where's my mom?" Murph immediately blurted into the handset.

There was a dry, rasping chuckle from the HALO unit. "Patience, patience, my friend. It's been a while since we saw each other, hasn't it? Let's get reacquainted. I'll start. Good evening, Kid Normal. It's so nice to speak to you again. Are you enjoying my little war? Is it keeping all you Heroes nice and busy? On your toes?"

Murph said nothing, gripping the handset so hard that his knuckles went numb. He refused to be toyed with like this.

"Don't feel like chitchat? Oh, very well," sighed Magpie's voice. The screen on the HALO unit flashed into life to reveal a picture that made Murph's insides shrivel. It was his mom's face, frozen in a look of terror.

"I sent a visitor to your house. Quite a large visitor. A prominent member of the Alliance of Evil, actually. One of my best people," went on Magpie in a maddeningly conversational tone of voice. "I think it's fair to say your mother may have been a little alarmed."

The screen now changed to a picture of Andy. He seemed to be shouting, and he was gripping the iron bars of a cell door.

"Your brother knows some rather unpleasant language, I'm sorry to say," Magpie continued mock-sadly. "But no matter. He'll soon learn some manners. They both will."

"Leave them alone!" Murph yelled furiously. He knew only too well what Magpie was capable of. The thought of his family at the mercy of this man filled him with rage and terror.

"Oh, I will," said Magpie softly. "As long as you do exactly what I tell you, Kid Normal." He spat the last two words out venomously.

Murph sank onto his bed, defeated. "Okay," he said dully. "What do you want?"

"Well, it's perfectly simple," came the voice in reply. "You are now on my side."

"What?" Murph scoffed before he could stop himself.

"Yes," gloated Magpie. "You're one of the bad guys now! How delicious! Now listen to me carefully. Every time you get sent on one of your precious Heroes' Alliance missions, that mission is going to fail. Do you understand me?"

"But . . . what . . . I can't just . . ."

"I said . . . do you understand me?" shouted Magpie, suddenly furious.

Murph's shoulders slumped. "Yes."

"Every mission you Super Zeroes go on is going to

go horribly wrong. Every Rogue you're sent to apprehend is going to escape. Every Alliance of Evil plan you try to thwart is going to mysteriously succeed. Or things will get very, very uncomfortable for your family. Got it?"

"Yes," mumbled Murph once again.

"Very good. I've decided it's time to swing the balance of the war a little. And just in case you get any clever ideas"— Magpie's voice was chilling now—"let me make this crystal clear. You tell nobody. Not your little Hero team, not your old friend the Blue Phantom, not her chauffeur. No one. Because make no mistake, my friend. I will find out. Immediately. And the consequences for your mother and brother will . . . not be pleasant."

"Fine," said Murph numbly.

"Make sure nobody meddles," continued Magpie. "No nosy neighbors, no one from that ridiculous school of yours. Nobody. Put the front door back on your house. Fend for yourself. It'll teach you a valuable lesson about life: you can't rely on anybody else."

There was a pause, and the screen on the HALO

unit reverted to its plain purplish glow. Then Magpie spoke once more.

"I'll be in touch again soon," he said, "to see how you're enjoying fighting for my side. You never know... You might actually rather like being a Rogue. Don't knock it until you've tried it—isn't that the expression? I'll be keeping a very close eye on your progress, so don't get any ideas about being a Hero, now, will you? You're on your own."

And with that, the HALO unit abruptly turned itself off.

Murph had no choice but to drag himself numbly down the stairs to try to repair his front door, feeling more alone than he ever had in his life.

11

Mega Melon

The first time Murph had seen the *Banshee* rolling out of Carl's garage on its fat black tires, jet engines gleaming in the sunlight, he had been so excited he thought his head might burst open like an overripe squash. The miraculous flying car had been a symbol of the whole hidden world of Heroes that was opening up to him. He could never have imagined that one day the sight of its silvery-blue fuselage would fill him with a sickening guilt and crushing anxiety.

And yet that day had come. When Nellie hovered beside his balcony to pick him up for a mission the following morning, his normal bubbles of anticipation had been replaced by a chilly, flat dread.

Now, as they soared above the autumn countryside, the muddy, plowed fields and skeletal trees forming a mournful, monochrome patchwork below them, Murph pressed his face to the window and clenched every muscle in it to stop the tears from forming. He felt like his insides had been removed, put into a blender, then replaced as a worry smoothie. Normally at this stage he'd be chatting with his friends about how they would triumph. Today he was silently brooding on how he could secretly make sure they failed.

"Earth to Murph!" He felt a friendly flick on the ear and turned to see Angel looking at him expectantly.

"Sorry . . ." he mumbled. "What?"

"Mission briefing about to come through. Weren't you listening?"

"I'm a bit tired," he explained dully. That at least was true. Murph had been up late with his mom's toolbox, fixing the front door as best he could. Then, after a dismal supper of cold beans, he'd lain awake for what was left of the night trying, and failing, to see any way out of his predicament.

"Super Zeroes receiving," Nellie was saying quietly into her headset. "On course for the coordinates provided. ETA fifteen minutes."

"Stand by," crackled a voice from the radio. Murph pinched himself hard on the leg, forcing himself to concentrate as he shuffled up to sit behind the pilot's chair.

"Banshee, come in. Super Zeroes, do you copy?" came a familiar voice over the speaker.

"Morning, Jasper!" answered Hilda happily.

"Ah, good morning, my horsey young friend! All ready for a mission, are we?"

Mary was looking at Murph expectantly. As their leader, he would normally have spoken up at this point, but today all he could do was stay glum and silent. So she filled in for him: "Zeroes standing by, Jasper. One of us would have liked to sleep in, by the look of it, but we're ready. What's the target?"

"Got an interesting one for you today, Zeroes," said Sir Jasper. "We have intelligence that a couple of members of the Alliance of Evil are planning a rather nasty attack. One of them caused quite a lot of trouble a few years back. He has a somewhat odd Cape . . . Basically, he can alter vegetables to make them into tranquilizers.

224

So he turns your dinner into knockout drops, then when you're unconscious . . . he robs you."

"Ooooh, *evil*," breathed Hilda.

"Sounds okay to me," Billy broke in. "Any excuse not to eat veggies. So this guy doctors vegetables. What's his name? The evil Doctor Vegetables?"

Mary laughed.

"Um, yes, as a matter of fact," Sir Jasper answered. "Doctor Vegetables is exactly what he's called."

"Villain names are boringly literal sometimes," huffed Hilda. "You'd think people would have more imagination."

"Anyhoo," Sir Jasper went on, "The Doctor has always worked with a chef called Monsieur Trois. And *his* Cape is . . . duplicating vegetables."

"Gross!" exclaimed Billy.

"They were both locked up in Shivering Sands, and now that they've escaped, it looks as if they're up to their old tricks again," Sir Jasper went on. "According to our tip-off, they're planning to contaminate an entire warehouse of vegetables . . . tonight. Your mission, should you choose to accept it, is to stop them! And even if you don't choose to accept it, that's still your mission. **Good luck! So long!"**

The radio fizzed and went dead.

"I always suspected that brussels sprouts were evil in some way," said Billy in a satisfied tone of voice as they started their descent. "I think we're about to prove it."

The *Banshee* touched down in a cobbled courtyard littered with stray bits of vegetables. Squished tomatoes, occasional mushrooms, and those leaves from the outside of cauliflowers that look like the wings of green bats were scattered everywhere.

"I think this could be the place," Mary whispered as they crept down the ramp.

"Oh, you think?" said Billy sarcastically, indicating the vegetable smorgasbord before them.

"I was being ironic," she informed him. "All right, Murph. What's the plan?"

"What?" Murph hadn't been listening. He was lagging behind, wondering desperately how he was supposed to sabotage their mission without letting anyone suspect he was doing it. He realized that his team was waiting for instructions. Usually this would be the time for what they called "Murph's Minute"—their moment of careful planning before they leaped into action. But his brain seemed frozen, paralyzed by his seemingly impossible task.

"Should I start, then?" said Mary, looking at him strangely. "Let's go through the risks. This Doctor person can make any vegetable into a tranquilizer. So the most important thing is: nobody eat any vegetables."

"This is already sounding like a mission I can get on board with," said Billy.

Hilda spoke next. "Maybe we should try to sneak in? See what we're up against. Murph?"

Again, Murph was silent.

"What's gotten into you?" Mary hissed.

He collected himself. He was going to have to make an attempt to seem normal, even though getting his brain to work felt like wading through quicksand.

"Right," he confirmed, twisting his face into some semblance of enthusiasm. "Yes, Hilda. Good. Sneak. Let's go." He headed off toward a large concrete loading ramp that led up to the back of the warehouse.

"That's it? That's the whole plan? Sneak?" he heard Mary whisper to Billy as they followed. "I don't know what's gotten into him today."

"Doctored sprouts, probably," replied Billy sagely.

The inside of the warehouse was cool and gloomy. The six of them crept down a long, sloping passageway littered with yet more vegetable debris, which made a slippery albeit vitamin-rich surface underfoot. They tried to keep as quiet as possible, though at one point Angel let out a small squeak as she lost her footing on a piece of cabbage. A bubble and squeak, in fact.

At the end of the hallway they could make out a greenish glow. As they cautiously approached the doorway, they could also hear a strange popping sound. Piles of pallets loaded with vegetables were stacked up just inside the main warehouse space, so the Super Zeroes and Angel were able to duck down and poke their heads around the corner to see what was going on.

A tall, thin man in a green top hat was standing in the center of the room. He was dressed in a strange collection of clothes: a bright yellow shirt, a pair of eggplant-colored Bermuda shorts, and large orange rain boots. His hair, which stuck out at all angles from beneath the top hat, was straw-colored, and his cheeks were rosy.

"Just a couple more, my friend," he was saying, "and I think that's shallot."

VEGETABLE PUNS—AN APOLOGY

We would like to apologize to any of our readers who may have an intolerance to vegetable-based puns. We realize that Doctor Vegetables just made an extremely bad pun on the phrase "That's your lot," referencing the popular mini-onion known as the shallot. If you thought this pun was offensive, then you may want to skip a few pages.

Murph, stuck at the back of the group, couldn't see who the man was talking to. Whoever it was had been obscured from view behind a large stack of wooden boxes—and that was where the popping noise was coming from.

"An entire warehouse full of knockout vegetables!" the man in the green top hat was now saying. "I am an über-genius!"

We did warn you.

Unfortunately (or fortunately if you're in a hurry for this chapter to be over), at that moment Mary leaned forward a little too far. She, too, was trying to see the other person in the room, but as she edged around the pile of pallets, it teetered and fell forward. Vegetables cascaded into the warehouse like an iron-enriched waterfall as the pallets clattered to the ground. Mary ended up spread-eagled on a carpet of carrots.

"Intruders!" shouted the man. **"Our secret lair is discovered! There must have been a leek! That's a turnip for the books!"**

Mary scrambled to her feet, the others moving out to join her. Murph dithered for a moment but decided that, for now at least, he would have to go along with whatever was about to happen.

"Doctor Vegetables, I presume,"

Mary was now saying in ringing tones.

"You clearly know your onions, young lady," the man replied, doffing his top hat and swooping into a low bow. A stray potato fell out of the hat and rolled across the floor.

"Put your hands up and come quietly," continued Mary sternly. "The game's up!"

"Don't be radish-ulous . . ." said

Doctor Vegetables slyly. "Not when my plan is about to come to fruition. We will pepper the town with my lovely knockout veggies! Then all we have to do is brocco-lie low until everybody is unconscious . . . and steal their valuables! We'll be millionaires this time tomato!"

"Technically that's a fruit," Mary retorted. "And it's a very low-quality pun anyway."

"Rhubarb!" spat Doctor Vegetables.

"Which, surprisingly, is actually a vegetable. Gold star," conceded Mary.

"Who knew?" Billy added.

"Mange-tout!" came a shout from off to one

side. And now the second villain stepped out from behind

231

the stack of boxes and came into view. Monsieur Trois was almost the exact opposite of Doctor Vegetables. Where the doctor was tall and thin, the chef was short and stout. In fact, he looked not unlike an apple in a chef's outfit. If you're having trouble imagining that, why not dress an apple in a small chef's outfit? That should give you the general idea.

"We are representatives of the Heroes' Alliance, and we demand that you surrender!" Mary shouted at him.

"*Quoi?*" the little man responded.

"Oh, jeez," said Mary. "Hang on. *Nous sommes . . .* um, *les . . .* What's French for 'representatives'?"

"Squash them, Monsieur Trois!" cried Doctor Vegetables. **"Butternut squash them!"** he added, just in case anybody had missed the subtlety of his latest pun. "Not one of them must be left a-chive!"

"*Oui, oui!*" replied Monsieur Trois, holding out his hands in a combat stance. And now the source of the noise they had heard became evident. With a sharp popping sound, the chef began firing baby carrots at

them like bullets. The Super Zeroes dived for
cover under the high-potassium onslaught.

Murph and Mary had
leaped to the left
and taken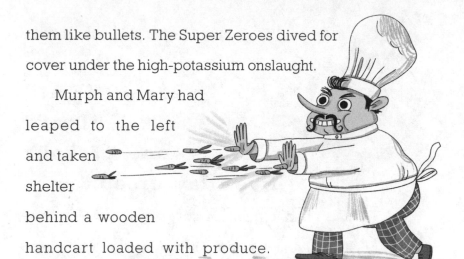
shelter
behind a wooden
handcart loaded with produce.
Billy, Nellie, Hilda, and Angel had
scattered to the right and were desperately trying to
find cover. Murph watched with his heart in his mouth
as Angel leaped into a forward roll to dodge a stream of
peas that were snapping into the stone wall behind her.
Magpie's words were sounding somewhere in the back
of his mind: *Every mission you Super Zeroes go
on is going to go horribly wrong*. But he couldn't
just abandon his friends in the middle of a battle. He
would have to work something out later.

"You know what this means?" Mary was shouting into
his ear. **"Food fight!"** She grabbed a cauliflower
from the cart, stood up, and lobbed it like a hand
grenade. It was a great shot—the knobbly white missile

hit Doctor Vegetables squarely in the face, sending him staggering backward. **"HA!"** exulted Mary. **"That's one of your five a day, creep!"** But she had to duck for cover again as Monsieur Trois sent a volley of high-velocity new potatoes at her.

By now Angel had scrambled to her feet, and she launched her own counter-attack. Mirroring Monsieur Trois's Cape, she sent a fusillade of sprouts pinging toward the chef, who reeled backward with a cry of ***"Choux-là-là!"*** He scampered away to regroup with Doctor Vegetables.

"Gotcha!" exalted Angel. **"Sprouts beat spuds every time! Eat my shorts!"**

"We really need to talk about her out-of-date slang," moaned Mary.

"And her out-of-whack taste in vegetables," shouted Billy, from behind a crate of melons.

"Think you've got me beet?" taunted Doctor Vegetables. "Think again! Time to send some of my knockout veg your way. Make sure you don't arti-choke on them!"

The two Rogues were now standing side by side and both raised their hands. A strange greenish glow surrounded Doctor Vegetables's fingers, and Monsieur Trois began firing more vegetables across the room—parsnips this time. But now the parsnips were all glowing with that odd green light.

"Knockout parsnips!" warned Mary—the first known use of that phrase ever in history. **"Keep your mouths shut!"**

"Keep up the pressure!" encouraged Hilda, who had armed herself with a container of tomatoes—a classic but ultimately messy weapon. She began to lob them over. Nellie joined in with a rain of zucchini; and Billy, who had discovered the warehouse's small but crucial fruit section, found that navel oranges made formidable cannonballs. By now, the room looked and smelled like the inside of a juicer in January.

Murph felt torn in two. This was exactly what he

loved—being in the thick of the action alongside his best friends. But all the same he knew that he had to make sure this mission didn't succeed. Every time a spark of euphoria sprang up as a well-aimed piece of fruit or a vegetable found its target, a wash of cold guilt extinguished it.

"Come on, Murph!" Hilda yelled over at him. "Grab a cabbage and get in on this!"

Murph was dithering over whether or not to reach out for a convenient cabbage when Billy decided to take matters into his own hands. He had grabbed an unusually large melon from the crate in front of him and was concentrating hard. With a huge, juicy **parp!** the melon inflated until it came up to his chest.

"Yeah!" he crowed, standing up and kicking the fruit so it started to trundle across the room toward their enemies. "See how you deal with that! **Super Melon!**"

Unfortunately, at that moment a well-aimed parsnip shot straight into his open mouth. A puff of green gas exploded around Billy's head, and he fell backward, knocked out cold.

"Oh, now you've got me really mad," fumed Angel,

throwing herself sideways with her hands outstretched.

"Mega Melon!" With an even

huger, juicier **parp!** the melon inflated once again.

Thanks to Angel's ability, it was now the size of a minivan. It

continued to pick up speed as it rolled across the room.

Doctor Vegetables and Monsieur Trois ran wildly

into a corner. "Why can't they just leave us in peas?"

moaned the doctor, followed by a single terrified shout

of **"Celery!"**—his puns finally deserting him as

the speeding melon found its target.

There was a gigantic *squelch* and a gentle rain of

sweet-scented juice. The Mega Melon cracked in two, and as the halves fell apart Murph could see that both Rogues had slumped to the floor. "Is everyone okay?" he asked urgently. "Nellie?"

She peeped in the affirmative.

"Angel?"

"Yip! All good."

"Hilda?"

"Victory!" cried Hilda, capering with joy, although slightly more gingerly than normal on the extremely slippery floor.

Mary was cradling Billy's head. "He seems okay," she told Murph. "He's just fast asleep. And he's going to be mortified when he wakes up and discovers he ate a parsnip."

"All right," decided Murph, as a plan began to form in his turbulent brain. "Mary, Angel—you two get Billy back to the *Banshee*. Nellie, go with them and prepare for takeoff. Hilda, let's get these two secure and report back."

In a side room, Murph and Hilda discovered an enormous safe filled with piles of jewelry, watches, and money: the spoils of Doctor Vegetables's earlier crimes. Working together, they managed to drag the two Rogues inside.

"Not mush-room in here, is there?" quipped Hilda excitedly. "Murph, did you hear? I did a veggie pun! I said . . . there's not *mush*—"

"Got it, got it. Nice one," said Murph, grinning in spite of himself. "Okay . . . You get in the *Banshee*. I'll lock this door and report back to the Alliance."

"Aye, aye, sir! I know things have been a bit strange between us all lately, but I bet now we're on the mend!" said Hilda chirpily, and skipped out of the room. "Another win for the Super Zeroes!" he could hear her saying to herself as she slopped back across the pulp-plastered warehouse. **"We are unstoppable!"**

Murph paused, one hand on the heavy safe door. More than anything else, Hilda's excitement had hit him like a punch to the stomach. Letting her down— puncturing her excitement and pride—would be the cruelest betrayal of all. Abruptly he swung the door closed and turned the metal wheel in the center, locking it tight. He had to do his duty as a Hero. He couldn't work against his friends. Perhaps he could still figure a way out of this without betraying them. But as he turned away, something caught his eye on the desk opposite.

It was a box full of those annoying little stickers you have to peel off apples. A pang of horrible sadness hit him. He and Andy had always used to try to sneak those stickers onto the back of their mom's sweater without her noticing. They were very good at it, too. A tear formed in the corner of his left eye as he thought of them both, locked up somewhere at Magpie's lair, not knowing where they were or why they had been captured.

Murph sighed. What choice did he have? Like a puppet controlled by an unfeeling master, he turned robotically back to the safe and spun the wheel in the other direction. The huge round door clanked and whirred as the bolts drew back. Murph pulled it open again, allowing light to flood back in and illuminate the two Rogues inside.

Doctor Vegetables, propped up against a pile of cash, was stirring. He raised a hand to shield his eyes, muttering, **"Wake up, you French bean!"**

Monsieur Trois gave a Gallic groan.

"You'd better get out of here," Murph told them flatly. "CAMU will be along soon."

Numbly he made sure that the door of the safe was firmly propped open so the two Rogues could escape as soon as they came to properly. Then, guilt and dread eating away at him like a worm gnawing at a nice juicy apple, he turned heavily on his heel and squelched away to re-join the friends he had just betrayed.

Murph Cooper wasn't particularly good at being bad. His whole work ethic was centered around saving the day—so un-saving it didn't come naturally to him. But Magpie kept up the pressure. The old HALO unit underneath Murph's bed would whisper to him in the night, demanding progress reports and flashing up constant reminders of what would befall his mom and Andy if he didn't cooperate or if he told anyone they had been kidnapped.

Unable to confide in anyone, Murph became more and more isolated and withdrawn as the days went by. His ears pricked up every time the HALO system crackled into life; he desperately hoped that the Heroes' Alliance would have Magpie cornered. But in his heart of hearts he knew that the man in black was too cunning, and his hopes sank further with each false alarm. Time and time again, Mary, or one of the other Super Zeroes, tried to find out what was making him so miserable. He always refused to talk about it, and with their missions going so badly, they all just assumed he was feeling frustrated about the Super Zeroes' failures.

And those failures kept on coming. Mission after mission ended in humiliation.

"It's almost as if you're trying to single-handedly lose this war for us," fumed Miss Flint two weeks later.

"We've actually got ten hands," proffered Billy helpfully. "Between all of us . . . you know."

The head of the Alliance glared at him. She was in no mood for nitpicking.

The five Super Zeroes had been summoned to Mr. Souperman's office during their lunch hour. Expecting the principal to greet them, they had been alarmed to find Miss Flint sitting stone-faced behind his large wooden desk, flicking through a thick hunk of papers. They knew all too well that they'd had a run of bad luck, but nobody had guessed that the head of the Alliance would personally fly in to give them a dressing-down.

The last time they had seen Miss Flint in person, she had been giving them the opposite of a dressing-down, whatever that is. A dressing-up? Or an undressing-down? Or an upward-dress-age? Whatever it was, it had been preferable to this. At Witchberry Hall, she had been telling the whole Heroes' Alliance what a shining example they were—a symbol of the new, open Alliance. A successful team of young Heroes, with a leader without a Cape. A model for how the Alliance could grow even stronger.

But today, things were very different.

"This file," she told them, slamming the thick papers down on the desk for emphasis, "is one of the most infuriatingly disappointing things I've ever read."

Four of the five Super Zeroes stared at Miss Flint in dismay. Only Murph quickly hung his head. He couldn't look her in the eye. He alone knew exactly who was to blame for the contents of this file.

"I simply cannot fathom how you've literally gone from Heroes to zeroes in such a short space of time," Miss Flint was now saying. "Perhaps I've been expecting too much of you . . . put too much pressure on you. Perhaps you weren't ready after all."

"We *were* ready!" Hilda piped up desperately. **"We *are*! We can get better!"**

"Well, you certainly can't get much worse," snapped their leader. "It all started going wrong after that Doctor Vegetables mess. What on earth happened there? He's been causing absolute havoc since then! And you told CAMU that he and Monsieur Trois were safely contained!"

"I—We—We don't know what happened there," stammered Mary. "When we left, they were safe in the . . . in the safe. Safely in the safe. I just don't get it."

"I just don't get it either, Mary Canary," said Miss Flint stonily. She picked up the file in front of her, then flicked through the pages and read some of the headings out loud.

"That wasn't our fault!" said Mary hotly. "We got a flat tire! We weren't able to chase them!"

"A bad worker blames their tools, Ms. Perkins," sniffed the head of the Alliance. She continued reading from the file:

"We got there too late," admitted Billy. "Remember, Murph? That's when you accidentally put in the wrong co-ordinates and we ended up at a completely different lake?"

Murph nodded silently. Miss Flint had turned to the next sheet in the file.

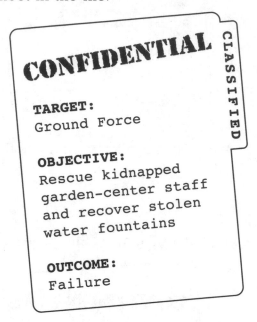

CONFIDENTIAL

CLASSIFIED

TARGET:
Ground Force

OBJECTIVE:
Rescue kidnapped garden-center staff and recover stolen water fountains

OUTCOME:
Failure

The five Super Zeroes stood in silence. There was no arguing with the facts. Presented in such stark terms, their current record, they had to admit, did not sound impressive.

"Outcome: Failure," Miss Flint went on, licking a thumb and shuffling through the rest of their recent missions. **"Outcome: Failure.**

Failure . . . Failure . . ." She glanced at the last sheet and shook her head as she read out the last word. **"Failure."**

An uneasy silence filled the room.

"At present, you're a danger to yourselves," Miss Flint resumed sharply. "A liability. We simply cannot allow you to become a danger to the public, or to the Alliance. You can consider this a final warning. **One more failed mission . . . and you're out."**

She slammed the folder closed.

Just a few days later, in the early hours of the morning, four members of the Super Zeroes awoke to the heart-clenching sound of their HALO units buzzing.

Billy read the message—SCRAMBLE IMMEDIATELY AND RENDEZVOUS WITH OTHER ALLIANCE UNITS: CRITICAL MISSION—and ballooned a knee in shock . . .

Nellie pushed her green-tipped hair out of her eyes and sighed with anxiety as she reached for the keys to the *Banshee* . . .

Hilda popped her horses into existence for an equine

pep talk: "Now, Artax, Epona . . . today we need to be at the very top of our game. So keep your heads up, eyes front, and best hooves forward!"

Mary checked and rechecked the action of her umbrella. She belted her raincoat with extra care. She polished her glasses, smoothed her scarf, and made sure she was ready for anything . . .

And it was all for one simple reason. This was their last chance.

Murph Cooper was the only Super Zero who wasn't woken by the buzzing of the HALO. He was already wide awake, in his empty house, when the call came in. Wiping away tears of anger and frustration from his eyes, he waited for the roar of the jet engines that would mean his friends had come to collect him for their mission.

The friends he was being forced to betray, coming to collect him for the make-or-break mission he would have to sabotage . . .

And that's more or less where we first came in, isn't it? Wasn't that dramatic? Thanks for bearing with us. We promise faithfully not to pull the whole "one month earlier" trick again in the next book. It's a "once in a series" kind of gambit.

So . . . you remember the first chapter, right? If not, here it is in fast-forward.

Super Zeroes, big exciting mission, stone circle, Druid, willow trees, horses, Murph sabotages it, Miss Flint kicks them out of the Alliance, they have a massive fight, Mary hears him talking to Magpie on the old HALO unit.

All right, all up to speed? Everyone ready for the next bit? Have you all been to the bathroom?

You haven't been to the bathroom? Oh, go on then. Be quick.

Okay, finished?

Did you wash your hands? Go back and wash your hands.

Have you done that? Did you use soap? Go and do them again.

Right. Good. Onward.

12

Murph Alone

"What happened to 'You don't need superpowers to be a hero'?" Murph Cooper asked quietly.

(We're back in the corridor at Witchberry Hall, outside Miss Flint's office. Remember? From the end of Chapter One? She's just thrown the Super Zeroes out of the Heroes' Alliance. But this time we're about to see the scene from Murph's point of view. It's very clever.)

Murph was hoping against hope that Mary, of all people, would understand. Surely she must know that he would never deliberately let his friends down? Surely she would work out that there was something else at play? Surely she hadn't lost that much faith in him?

"Well, maybe you do need them, Murph. Maybe you do."

Mary's words hit him with such force, it was as if

he was suddenly seeing the world through a pane of glass. Like a part of his brain had closed itself off to protect him from the hurt he'd feel if he fully processed what Mary had just said.

Before he was fully aware of what was happening, his legs were carrying him away from the rest of the Super Zeroes, through a heavy wooden door, and out into an ornamental garden.

The clear, sunny day was turning into a cold evening, and the grass and shrubs were already thick with frost. Murph's breath billowed in clouds ahead of him as he stumbled numbly around hedges and down gravel pathways, eventually sinking onto a wooden bench and plunging his head into his hands.

He wasn't sure how long he'd been sitting there, but when Magpie's voice rang out through the frozen air Murph's hands were numb with cold. It was a struggle to get the old HALO unit out of his jeans pocket and answer.

"Are you there, Kid Normal?"

"Yes," Murph answered crossly. "I'm here, I'm here. What do you want now? The Super Zeroes are finished.

We've been kicked out of the Alliance. I can't sabotage any more missions for you. It's over."

"It's not over, Kid Normal. Not by a long shot. Not until I say so. But first—I want you to tell me more about the mission. Did you succeed in your task today?"

"Yes." A great weariness was settling on Murph. The enormity of what he had done was seeping through. "I managed to sabotage the mission. I disabled the electronics in the vehicles with a TEMP unit."

"Splendid," gloated Magpie. "Really, really splendid. My associate was able to escape, and I hear he has something rather special planned that will keep those fools in the Heroes' Alliance on their toes. Little suspecting that you are right in their midst . . ."

As Magpie went on, reveling in his victory, Murph thought he heard a rustling, crunching noise behind him. He even looked around, absurdly hoping that perhaps Mary had come to find him, but could make out no shape in the twilight. Surely he'd just imagined the flash of yellow among the topiary.

He couldn't bear any more of Magpie's gloating. **"I'm not in their midst anymore,"** he interrupted. **"I told you, we've been kicked out."**

Magpie's croaky voice sounded unsurprised. "And how did your so-called friends deal with that news. Were they sympathetic toward you, I wonder? Understanding and kind? Or did they blame you . . . ?"

An unwelcome thought came to Murph, flapping into his mind like an errant bat into a summer bedroom. *What if some missions had just gone wrong by accident?* it whispered to him. *What if it hadn't been your fault at all? Would Mary still have said that to you? Aren't you the perfect scapegoat? When the chips are down . . . will they always look to you as the weak link in the chain? Because you're the boy without a Cape . . . ?*

Magpie almost seemed to hear this thought as if he had spoken it out loud. Murph felt once again that uncomfortable sensation he had encountered the first time he'd visited the cell in Shivering Sands— a feeling like countless metallic wings thrumming the air around him. *He understands what it's like to be an outsider*, the unwelcome voice in his head murmured.

"I think it's time to answer the crucial question, don't you?" said the voice of Magpie.

Murph's skin crawled. "What?" he asked.

"Do you still believe that you can be a Hero without powers? Your friends certainly don't seem to think so, now, do they? So consider your answer carefully. Do you need superpowers to be a Hero?"

Murph thought for a moment. "I honestly don't know anymore," he replied, exhausted and defeated. **"I certainly don't have what it takes. So, maybe you do. Yes."**

"Excellent," purred Magpie quietly, "I think you're ready. Ready to leave the world of Heroes behind. It is time. Time for you to enter the Shadow Machine."

The HALO unit emitted a shrill double beep that Murph had never heard before. Glancing down at the screen he saw the letters spelling COORDINATES RECEIVED scrolling across it.

Murph's mind felt fogbound. But one thought came to him very clearly. Whatever trap Magpie was luring him into, whatever twisted torture machine he might have created . . . he had given away his location. And wherever Magpie was, surely Murph's mother and brother must be there too. It was something to cling on to, at least. "I'm on my way," he told the handset, scrambling to his feet.

"So eager." Magpie chuckled. "Excellent. And I think you know where you can find a vehicle to get you here."

Murph remembered Carl's story about the night Angel had faced Magpie and knew exactly what he had to do. Angel had been blundering into the unknown; he would be going fully aware of what he was about to face. But there was no other option.

After all, he thought to himself sadly, remembering Mary's stinging words, *there's nothing left for me here.*

Murph had been prepared for a degree of sneaking around, or some fast-talking at the very least, but the main workshop inside Witchberry Hall was deserted. A few lights had been left on above workbenches, but otherwise the room was dim. His footsteps sounded gigantic as he clanged down the stairs and made his way over to the far end of the room. Grasping a corner of a large white cloth, he pulled it sharply to one side.

The silvery metal sides of the *Wyvern* caught the reflection of a nearby lamp. Gulping, Murph reached out and flicked the switch on the control panel. There was a high-pitched whine as the bike's electrical systems charged up, and the main screen lit up: **WYVERN READY.**

Murph steeled himself and threw a leg over the fat leather saddle. Pulling the old HALO unit out of his pocket, he held it near the dashboard, not certain how the technology would work but sure that Carl would have designed these two systems to work together. Sure enough, there was a tone from the handset and an answering bleep from the *Wyvern*. The message on the screen changed: **COORDINATES RECEIVED.**

A single red button on the left handlebar had begun flashing. Holding his breath, Murph pushed it with a thumb. Then several things happened at once.

There was a massive grinding from the hangar doors above him as they began to roll open. There was a roar from the *Wyvern* as its twin engines flared into life. And there was a click and a whine as two slim silver wings extended on either side of the fuel tank.

Hang on, thought Murph to himself. *Whatever you do, hang on.*

The roar rose to a scream—so loud that Murph could not hear the clanging of a pair of black boots rushing down the metal stairs.

The motorcycle shuddered, then shook, then shot skyward—so fast that Murph could not turn to see the arms of a yellow raincoat waving frantically at him.

Within seconds the *Wyvern* was nothing more than a fast-moving silver speck between the stars. The flying umbrella that had tried desperately to follow in its wake was left behind, its owner drifting disconsolately down and back through the hangar doors of Witchberry Hall.

13

The Silence of the Weasel

Sir Jasper Rowntree had been rather enjoying his retirement. Lazy mornings with the crossword, some occasional tinkerings with the many vintage Hero vehicles in his workshop, and perhaps a cup of tea with his friends Flora and Carl and a chat about the old days. Until recently he would have been nodding by the fire with a milky drink by this time of night—but now instead he was trying to coordinate the resources of the entire Heroes' Alliance. And not a mug of hot chocolate in sight. War didn't make allowances for bedtime beverages.

"Can't we send any more units to cover the docks? No? We've had a confirmed sighting of Goldfish!" he said into his headset. **"Vapor Trail? Come in, Vapor Trail!"**

"We've got the situation at the zoo contained," said

a voice over the speakers in his office. "No, wait. What's that? Defensive positions!" There was a loud bleating in the background.

Sir Jasper rolled his eyes. The Alliance of Evil, emboldened by The Druid's escape that morning, was stretching the Heroes to breaking point. A barrage of attacks throughout the day had seen team after team of Heroes dispatched in a desperate attempt to head off the onslaught. He was now one of the few Alliance operatives left at Witchberry Hall, trying frantically to coordinate several different operations single-handed. The last thing he needed was the one team of Heroes he couldn't send into action bursting through his door in a blind panic.

Mary, Nellie, Hilda, and Billy burst through Sir Jasper's door in a blind panic.

"We need to speak to DoomWeasel, now!" Mary was yelling. "You have to tell us where he is."

"What the hairy heck are you all up to?" the old man blurted out.

"Trying to tamp down this invasion of evil alpacas, of course!" came the voice of Vapor Trail over the radio, to the accompaniment of more bleating and spitting noises.

"No, no, not you . . ." Sir Jasper flicked a switch and the speaker went silent. He took his headset off, wiped a bead of sweat off his brow, and produced an exhausted half smile, half sigh.

"It's chaos out there, and we simply don't have enough agents to go around," he explained. "Colonel Flash is the only one who seems to be loving it. Giant lunatic keeps calling me on the HALO asking for another mission. The Ex-Cape Committee have been called out and I've just this minute had to mobilize Miss Flint herself. But what's the rush with you red-faced young shrimp? I heard you'd been let go!"

"We have been let go," confirmed Mary, **"but Miss Flint didn't know the full story, none of us did!** Our missions have been failing, it's true, but only because Murph was sabotaging them!"

"What? What the holy heck are you saying?" Sir Jasper rolled his chair forward, his brow furrowed with concern. "Murph's been kiboshing your missions? Why?"

It was the exact question Mary had been asking herself as they pelted through the hall toward this control room: Why?

"I don't know," she admitted.

"Magpie must be forcing him," broke in Hilda decisively. "Murph would never let us down unless he was being made to."

"Of course not," Mary said, but without conviction. Clouds of doubt were crowding her mind, stopping her from thinking straight. Over and over again she kept reliving her stinging words to Murph from earlier. She had told him that maybe he did need a Cape. Then he'd been speaking to Magpie about some kind of machine . . . Her scalp crawled with guilt and fear.

"Where is young Kid Normal, anyway?" Jasper was asking.

"That's just it . . . he's gone," said Mary, pulling herself together. "He's gone to Magpie, and we need to follow him. That's why we need your help."

"Hang on, hang on. Just hold your tiny horses for a tweed-weaving minute," pleaded Sir Jasper, waving his hands. "Are you saying you actually have a lead on Magpie's location? If Murph's gone to join him . . ."

"Face him," corrected Hilda. **"Murph would never join Magpie."**

"Well, whatever he's gone for, surely we can track him through his HALO?"

"Miss Flint took our HALOs," wailed Hilda.

"And that's why we need DoomWeasel," finished Mary. **"There's no time to lose. He must know where Magpie is."**

The idea had come to her as they raced through the corridors after she had failed to stop Murph. Mary Perkins hated loose ends. If she went to someone's house and there was a half-finished jigsaw on the table, her fingers started to twitch. And she had suddenly realized there was someone at Witchberry Hall who could be the missing piece to their current puzzle.

"DoomWeasel?" The old man wrinkled his already-quite-wrinkled brow. "But he's been questioned multiple times by the best minds in the Alliance. He's refusing to say anything."

"He may have refused to talk to the best minds

in the Alliance," said Mary, her eyes lighting up, "but there's one group of people who definitely know how to dig up embarrassing information about teachers. And that's schoolchildren."

"Well . . ." Sir Jasper mused. "I don't see the harm. If you can really get him to talk . . . it would be the breakthrough we've all been waiting for. All right! I'll stay here, put out the emergency call, and as soon as some missions have finished, we'll call as many Alliance units as we can muster back here and get a strike force together." He reached over and tapped at the HALO screen fastened to one arm of his electric wheelchair. "In the meantime, I'm giving you clearance for the cellblock. It's underneath the West Wing."

Without pausing, Mary and the others dashed out of the control room and were off.

"Which way is the West Wing?" shouted Mary as they dashed down the flagstoned passageway.

"West?" proffered Billy helpfully.

"Yeah, thanks," replied Mary a trifle irritably. "But

which is that? Why don't they just call them the Left Wing and the Right Wing?"

"Because that would depend on which way you were facing to start with," argued Hilda sensibly.

"It's over there," broke in Nellie, pointing to their right. **"Ooh, the human compass!"** exclaimed Hilda. "That's awesome. How did you know that?"

"I saw the sign," said Nellie's gentle voice. She was pointing at a small sign on the wall that read, "West Wing: Kitchens, Armory, Cellblock", underneath a large, clear arrow.

"Well, yes, you could always cheat, I suppose," said Mary huffily as they charged off in that direction.

Even with the entire fighting force of the Alliance out on missions, the cellblock could never be left completely unattended. At the bottom of a wide stone staircase was a large metal door with a barred window in the center. Just beside this was another, open wooden door in the wall, and Mary could see two armed Cleaners sitting rigidly on chairs inside—evidently this was a guardroom. On the other side of the passageway was a desk with a third Cleaner sitting behind it, tapping at a computer terminal.

"We want to see DoomWeasel," demanded Mary. **"We've got clearance."**

The Cleaner tapped her keyboard, and the terminal emitted a small **bing!** "You do have clearance," she confirmed in a serious voice. "Very well, then. He's in the last cell on the right. You can't miss it. Stay in the middle of the passageway on your way down, and don't look to the right or left. When you get to his cell, do not touch the glass—do not approach the glass."

"Why not?" Hilda wanted to know.

"Because I have just cleaned the glass, and I don't want kids' sticky fingerprints all over it," answered the Cleaner impassively, pushing a button. There was a metallic buzzing, then a clanking, and the metal door slid to one side to reveal a small block of eight cells.

"Last cell on the right," remembered Mary, and led the others to the far end of the block.

The guard wasn't wrong. You couldn't mistake the cell. In fact, you could smell it before you got to it.

If you've ever owned a hamster, you'll find DoomWeasel's cell quite easy to visualize. If you have never owned a hamster, imagine what it would have been like to own a hamster before you move on to the next paragraph. Pick a color for your hamster. Now give it a name. What did you go for? We've imagined a blue hamster called Clarice McWhirlpool. Anyway— now imagine your hamster chews stuff up and uses it to decorate its little cage. Toilet paper rolls, bits of wood, paper. Anything. **Chew chew chew, scrabble scrabble scrabble. ALL NIGHT LONG. Aaaargh! SHUT UP, CLARICE McWHIRLPOOL! WHY ON EARTH DID I BUY A NOCTURNAL PET! I NEED TO SLEEP! I HATE YOU! HAMSTERS ARE THE WORST!**

Sorry.

We got carried away there with our imaginary hamster, Clarice McWhirlpool. But what we're getting at is . . . You know the way hamsters chew lots of stuff up and fill their cages with it? That's what DoomWeasel had done, only with trash. His cell, which was a large room with a wide glass window at the front, was almost full of mashed-up cardboard boxes, food containers, and bits of a mattress that had been pulled apart so the stuffing went everywhere.

It looked like a giant hamster cage. And it smelled like one too.

The Super Zeroes lined up in front of the window like visitors at the zoo trying to spot the red pandas, which are always hiding. (Because they are evil. Don't tell anyone we told you that.)

"Where is he?" whispered Nellie, but Mary was in no mood to wait. She was convinced that the man in this cell held the key to tracking down their leader and friend, and she wasn't going to hang around until feeding time.

"Drench!" she hollered at the top of her voice, hammering on the window with the flat of her hand.

"Hey!" came the Cleaner's voice from the other end of the cellblock. **"I distinctly told you not to touch the glass!"**

"DRENCH!" yelled Mary again. There was a disturbance in the middle of the cell, as if an animal of some sort was moving about underneath the stinking debris. And then, abruptly, a head popped out of the muck like a seal coming up for air from a polluted pool.

DoomWeasel, previously known as Mr. Drench, looked—if possible—even crazier than before. His round glasses were smeared and bent, his hair was wild and unkempt, and there was a rat sitting on his head, preening its whiskers.

"Who's there?" he piped suspiciously. "I can't see! I'm blind!"

"Clean your glasses," said Mary impatiently. "They're filthy."

DoomWeasel took off his glasses and wiped them on the sleeve of his tattered old tweed jacket before putting them back on. He peered through the window. "Visitors! I wasn't told I would have visitors. **Have you come to marvel at my powers?"**

"We have come to get some answers out of you," said Mary curtly, "and your powers are not very impressive. If, by 'powers,' you mean shredding up a comforter and making a total mess of your cell."

"Mess . . . ha ha, yes, mess." DoomWeasel drooled. "The things you Heroes discard. The unwanted, the

outcast. These shall forever be my home. My guardians and protectors, as the great Ratsputin and I plot the overthrow of the Heroes." He giggled, coughing halfway through and spitting out a feather.

"*Meep*," added Ratsputin, sitting back on his haunches.

"Look, we don't have time for this," broke in Mary. "If you are plotting the overthrow of anything, it's bath time, because you smell. Now listen to me. Magpie doesn't respect you. He doesn't think you're a supervillain. He thinks you're an idiot."

"Lies!" hissed the little man, suddenly burrowing back underneath the trash and resurfacing right by the window. His large eyes, magnified by his still-filthy glasses, stared at them. "My master knows—"

"Your master?" broke in Mary scornfully. "You even call him your master! You've just turned into a sidekick all over again!"

"I am not a sidekick!" raged DoomWeasel, shedding rat droppings from the folds in his clothes as he shook with anger. **"I am the MAIN kick! I am . . ."**

"Mr. Drench," Hilda finished for him kindly. "You

are Mr. Drench, and you were our teacher. And a good teacher, actually."

Mary turned, eyebrows raised to critical levels. *What are you doing?* she mouthed at Hilda.

"I just thought . . ." Hilda whispered. "Everyone's been so horrible to him, for years and years. I wondered whether, you know . . . we should try being kind to him for once."

Mary's face dropped. Hilda was absolutely right. She was so desperate for answers that she'd been trying to bully them out of him. Perhaps the one thing DoomWeasel would respond to was some simple respect.

"Mr. Drench?" Mary began again.

"Drench?" squeaked the little man. **"That name no longer has any meaning for me. DoomWeasel is evil! DoomWeasel is powerful! DoomWeasel tears his comforter into little pieces to make his cell nicer."**

"Weeek," agreed the rat perched amid his wispy white hair.

"DoomWeasel," said Hilda gently, moving forward and placing her hand on the glass in a friendly gesture, "is the worst villain ever. Not to mention the least hygienic."

"Whereas Mr. Drench," Mary added in a soothing voice, "has helped literally hundreds of children master their Capabilities."

The man in the cell was looking at her with a strange expression, as if he was recalling a buried memory or hearing something a very, very long way away.

"DoomWeasel," Mary continued, "is very bad at being bad. Mr. Drench, on the other hand, is good. And the Heroes' Alliance should have been better at telling him that."

"They disregarded me!" squeaked DoomWeasel.

"That's right," agreed Mary. "They didn't pay you enough attention. Nobody did. And nobody told you that they liked you, or that they were grateful for you taking the time to teach them about Capabilities. But *we* are grateful. Thank you, Mr. Drench. Thanks for being our teacher."

"Yeah, she's right," realized Billy. "You looked after the kids with weird Capes like mine. Not just the cool kids. Thanks, Mr. Drench."

"Thanks," added Nellie softly, smiling up at the teacher through her green-tipped hair.

"You told us about the Blue Phantom," remembered Hilda. "We wouldn't have defeated Nektar without that information. Thanks, Mr. Drench."

A tear was collecting at the corner of DoomWeasel's eye. It had started off clear, but by the time it had trickled its way to his chin it had turned a rich brown color, like a tiny potato. It was the first time any part of the teacher's face had been washed in months.

"The Alliance and The School should have appreciated you more. But Magpie's much, much worse," Mary told him. "He's been using you. He calls you an idiot. He's only out for himself . . . and now he's got our friend."

"He did call me an idiot," DoomWeasel remembered sadly. "Seventy-eight times in total. I was counting."

"Smeep," agreed Ratsputin.

"We can stop him," said Mary. "But only if you help us. We need to know where he is."

DoomWeasel took off his glasses and wiped his eyes, leaving wide streaks down both sides of his filthy face.

After a moment, he put his glasses back on. His eyes were as large as ever behind their lenses, but Mary could now see that they had lost their manic gleam. They looked sad, and tired.

"You will defeat him?" he asked Mary quietly.

"You know it," she replied.

"And can I keep the rat?"

"Pinkie swear," answered Mary solemnly.

Mr. Drench nodded. "Very well," he sighed. "I shall tell you where Magpie is."

"Yes!" Hilda clapped her hands. **"We're off to rescue Murph! Mr. Drench, you are a total HERO!"**

And a smile, rare as a sponge, lit up the little man's face.

14

The Pilot Light

The sky darkened to a somber, dirty royal blue as Murph Cooper flew toward his enemy. The cold wind stung his eyes and froze his hands to the *Wyvern*'s handlebars as the landscape rushed past far below him. And as the afternoon was dragged toward the horizon by the clutching orange fingers of evening, a single star became visible, held inside a tattered frame of cloud.

He had no idea what he was flying toward. He had no plan for what to do when he got there. He had lost his friends. He had lost his status as a Hero. But something about that lone, ancient star gave him a strange, tiny flicker of courage and hope. It planted one particular memory in his mind as the motorcycle began, imperceptibly at first, to lose height.

It had been a few years earlier, and the hot water in their house had gone off. Andy had been upstairs trying to run a bath, and his mom had been using seven-year-old Murph as an assistant as she tried to fix the boiler. He had always loved helping his mom out, handing over the right tool from her enormous toolbox and watching as she used it expertly on whatever problem she was solving.

"These are the burners, in here," his mom had been saying to him as they shivered in the cold, brightly lit kitchen. "The gas comes in here"— she had pointed with the end of a screwdriver—"and then it catches fire to heat the water. And at the back there, there should be a pilot light."

"What's a pilot light?" Murph had wanted to know. He liked the sound of it. He knew a pilot led the way for other boats at the port near their house, so he imagined that a pilot light must be something that showed you where to go.

"A pilot light is a light that never goes out," his mom had explained. "At least it shouldn't. It's tiny, and it's always burning out of sight, ready to start everything working. But it's too bright in here to see if ours has gone out or not. We need to do this."

Murph's mom had reached out and flicked the light switch up, plunging the chilly kitchen into darkness. "Look," he heard her say, and felt her arms pick him up from behind and lift him up to look inside the boiler.

There, only just visible, was a tiny blue glow. "That's the pilot light," his mom told him, setting him back down on the tiled floor. "And now that we know that it's on, we can try doing this and see what happens . . ." She was fiddling with one of the pipes under the boiler, and suddenly there was a soft *whumph* of igniting gas. "Voilà!" she exclaimed, grinning.

"Hot water!" came Andy's delighted voice from upstairs.

"Good job, assistant plumber!" Murph's mom had congratulated him, solemnly shaking him by the hand as he beamed with pride.

Now, five years later, Murph wondered why that particular scene had come into his mind. Was he, he pondered, simply remembering a happy, secure time far away from his current situation? Or was there something buried deep inside his brain trying to give him a message?

"You can only see whether the pilot light's still on when things are at their darkest . . ." he murmured to himself softly. **"When all other lights go out."**

His ears popped painfully as the *Wyvern* sped diagonally downward toward its destination.

Murph's mom was not aware she'd just been the subject of a touching memory twenty miles away. And even if she had known that, she'd have been far too furious to care.

"You . . ." she was screaming at Magpie, and then she added a few very un-parent-like words that we couldn't possibly tell you in a fun, cuddly book like this.

Magpie raised his eyebrows slightly, but otherwise gave no reaction. "Please try to control yourself, Ms. Cooper," he told her in his infuriatingly calm, smug voice.

The room where Murph's mom and brother were being held was damp and cold. Not unlike a low-budget hotel, only with a much better lock and no tea- or coffee-making facilities. Its barred door looked out on a platform above the huge control room where the Shadow Machine was located.

Over the past two weeks, Murph's mom had watched the black-coated man and his oily, shiny-shoed friend carefully as they tinkered with their strange metal pyramid. She was trying desperately to work out why they were holding her prisoner. Andy had alternated between sulking and sleeping, but as he was a teenager this wasn't especially unusual.

So far the pair of them had been taken care of reasonably well, though their food and drink was brought to them by a bewildering series of characters, including a pig in a suit, who had cooked them a surprisingly nice moussaka. Even the man in the shiny shoes had come up once or twice at first, though he seemed to have been keeping a low profile over the past day or two. But this was the first time the man in black himself—the one who was obviously in charge of this bewildering place—had come to talk to her, and Katie Cooper was not going to miss the opportunity to give him a large slice of her mind, with a side order of nice, steaming-hot I-hate-you.

"Why are you keeping us prisoner, you mangy old crow? What have we done? **I want a phone call. I want a lawyer! I want you to get your horrible straggly hair cut!**"

"This will all be over very, very soon," Magpie continued, appearing not to have heard her. "Your other son should be arriving any minute now."

"Murph? What's Murph got to do with any of this?" raged Katie.

"I'm afraid you need to prepare yourself for something of a shock, my dear lady." taunted Magpie. "You see"—he pulled a large phone handset out of his pocket—"young Murph is not all he seems to be."

He held out the phone so she could see the screen. It was showing the feed from a camera inside one of the enormous concrete chimneys outside. And against the backdrop of stained and pitted gray, Katie could see a motorcycle . . . somehow suspended in the air. It was slowly coming in to land, and the figure sitting astride the machine was unmistakable.

"Whoa . . ." Andy had come forward to peer through the bars beside her. "A . . . flying motorcycle. You know what this means, Mom?"

"I have literally no idea what any of this means," said Katie blankly.

"Murph . . . is a wizard,"

breathed Andy.

"Of course he isn't a wizard, you stupid child," snapped Magpie angrily. "There aren't wizards." He collected himself with some difficulty. "But there is a great deal more that you do not know about your brother. You are about to learn many, many secrets about Murph Cooper.

And so are the Heroes who look up to him. Fools!"

Whirling his tattered black coat behind him, he stalked down a black spiral staircase toward the Shadow Machine. Once in the main chamber, he moved across to the wall and began adjusting a large camera.

*

"Come on . . . come on . . ." said Mary anxiously, peering across the dark garden from the *Banshee*'s ramp.

"Preflight checks complete," came Nellie's voice from the cockpit.

"And co-pilot in position and ready!" added Billy from the seat beside her.

"Hurry up," urged Mary. There was no time to spare. She let out a gasp of relief when a strip of light showed that the door to Witchberry Hall had opened. Two shadowy figures could now be seen racing toward the car, one dragging the other by the hand.

"I've found her!" came Hilda's voice from one shadow. **"She was in the library."**

"Yeah, kicking my heels, wondering if anyone was going to offer me a lift home," said the other shadow. It was Angel. Mary saw her silvery hair glint in the *Banshee*'s landing lights as she arrived at the ramp and stood before them, hands on hips. "Mom and Dad have jetted off on a mission, leaving me behind as usual. Well? What's going on? Horsey Hilda says something's up."

Hilda scuttled past her and into the flying car.

"Murph's gone," said Mary. "We're going to find him, and . . . and I want you to come with us."

"To be honest," replied Angel, "I haven't really had the impression you were that happy about me tagging along with you in the past."

"That's true," Mary said quietly, "I was blaming you for things that had nothing to do with you really, and I'm sorry. Turns out that Magpie's been behind this all along."

"WHAT?"

"And that's where Murph's gone."

"But you need to tell the Alliance!" Angel blustered.

"We have," said Mary urgently. "We told Jasper and he's recalling as many Heroes as he can to form an attack plan. But that could take ages! We need to get there NOW and stop Murph from . . . whatever he's trying to do. Look what happened to you when you tried to take on that maniac on your own!"

Angel thought for a moment. "I'm guessing you've been expressly forbidden from doing anything like this?" she said tentatively.

"Oh yes," confirmed Mary. "I've promised Jasper faithfully that we're going to wait for backup."

Slow grins spread over both girls' faces as they realized that they were, and always had been, on the same team.

"So what do you say?" asked Mary. "Murph Cooper rescue mission on?"

"Secret, non-Alliance-sanctioned, incredibly dangerous Murph Cooper rescue mission?" clarified Angel.

"Oh, heck yes, all those things." "Then slip me some skin, sister!"

Angel held up a hand ready for a high five.

"I don't know what that means," confessed Mary. "But if you're coming, then let's go!"

Angel scrambled into the cockpit after her.

"We must be ages behind him already. How long's the flight?" Hilda asked grimly as the *Banshee* lifted off from the herb garden.

"Looks like about an hour," replied Billy, glancing at the *Banshee*'s control panel, where a map showed the location of Titan Thirteen.

"It might take an hour normally," came a soft voice from the pilot's chair, "but not today." Nellie was tapping on the central HALO screen with one hand and flicking switches with the other. "You're going to want to buckle up," she told the rest of the Super Zeroes. "I've never done this before—Carl says it's too noisy unless it's a total emergency."

"This is a total emergency," Mary informed her.

"I know," replied Nellie simply. **"So buckle up. Now!"**

They scrambled for position. Billy pulled a webbing harness down around his chest. The others braced themselves against the back wall of the cockpit, where Carl had installed some simple lap belts at floor level above a few ancient-looking cushions, and made themselves as secure as they could. All the while the car was rising rapidly, rocking slightly as it crossed streams of wind on the way up.

"I think that's high enough," murmured Nellie to herself, inspecting the instrument panel. "Right—hang on. **We're going supersonic."** She eased the throttle forward and pressed a switch on one side of the lever that allowed it to go farther than normal. The usual scream of the *Banshee*'s engines rose to an even higher pitch, and they were all pressed backward hard by the g-force.

"I feel like a dog with its head out of the car window," complained Billy, grimacing.

Suddenly, there was an enormous bang from outside.

"Did we break something?" gasped Billy in alarm.

"Yep," answered Nellie, grinning slightly in spite of herself. "The sound barrier. **Titan Thirteen, here we come!"**

15

Twilight of the Super Zeroes

The *Wyvern* kicked up plumes of chalky gray dust as it landed inside the huge chimney. Murph let go of one of the handlebars and covered his mouth with his sleeve as the bike settled on the ground. Its screen displayed the message **OBJECTIVE REACHED.**

He dismounted and looked around. The concrete walls curved upward dizzyingly all around him. And over on one side was a single open door. Clearly that was the way Magpie wanted him to go. And it must be where Mom and Andy were being held. Swallowing, Murph walked through it.

He found himself in a long, brick passageway that connected the chimney with the main buildings of the power plant. The floor here was cleaner, and his footsteps echoed eerily as he made his way to the archway at the other end. Even before he reached it, he knew that Magpie would be waiting for him on the other side. A purplish glow was emanating from the large room.

"Come in, come in, don't be shy."

Magpie's coaxing voice rang out through the archway.

Murph stepped into the room. He could see the man in black standing expectantly beside a huge metal structure in the middle of the space. The last light of sunset was shining through the large, dirty glass dome in the center of the ceiling, but it was not enough to dull the purple glow that was coming from the platform on top of the flattened pyramid. Murph peered through the metal grills that formed the sides of the machine at the quietly turning gears inside.

He could feel a strange atmosphere in the air. There was an oppressive heaviness around the metal pyramid—a sultry crackle like the sensation you get on a hot summer's day and know that a massive storm is brewing.

Magpie was wearing the mocking smile Murph remembered so well. He seemed relaxed, Murph thought, not poised for attack. But it gave Murph no comfort. He was all too aware that the calmer Magpie appeared, the more dangerous he was.

"Where's my mom? Where's Andy?" he demanded furiously.

"Murph!" came a shout from an iron platform overhead.

Murph knew better than to lose sight of his enemy. Without taking his eyes off Magpie he asked, "Are you both okay?"

"We're fine," his mom replied. "Not leaving this place a great review online though."

Murph smiled.

"Oh, how very touching," Magpie jeered, his face contorting with contempt.

"I'll give you *touching*," came Murph's mom's furious voice, "I'll do more than touch you when I get out of here. I'll—"

Magpie gestured with a finger, and a wall of purplish light appeared in front of the platform, cutting off all sound from the cell.

"That's better."

Murph could almost feel the hatred washing

outward from Magpie's thin figure like a wave of freezing cold air. He shivered involuntarily, thinking of the array of Capes that were now ranged against him. If this was going to be a battle, it was one he could not hope to win. In coming here, he had already admitted defeat.

Nellie pulled back on the throttle, and the *Banshee* began to lose height as it eased down through thick wads of dark cloud. Soon they were flying low over deserted hills, and as they rounded one stark and craggy peak, two massive gray chimneys came into view. They were chipped and stained with years of disuse, but the left-hand one was pouring white steam into the air.

Beside the chimneys was a wide area dotted with metal pylons, thick electrical wires strung between them. In the dull light Mary could see that the wires were pulsing and sparking an unwholesome purple: a color that filled her heart with a cold dread. It was the same color as the forks of lightning that Magpie used to suck away the powers of Heroes. It was the color of fear, and of hate.

"That's it," she said quietly. "That's where he's got Murph."

Hilda reached over and squeezed her shoulder. **"Not for long,"** she reassured her.

The control panel beeped. "We've picked up the *Wyvern's* signal!" said Nellie, bringing the car in to land as quietly as possible inside the second great chimney. The jets kicked up clouds of chalky dust, but the motorcycle that had carried Murph here was still plain to see.

"All right," Mary told the others as the ramp extended. "Everyone ready?"

"Equana ready," began Hilda, before adding, "Oh, hang on. We're not in the Alliance any more, are we? I can't use that name—I'm not a Hero." Her face fell.

"You are every inch a Hero," Mary told her. "And your name doesn't change that."

"Right." The dusty air swirled as her red curls tossed defiantly. **"Hilda ready!"**
"Nellie ready," confirmed Nellie softly, though Mary could feel that the hand gripping tightly on to her left arm was shaking with fear.

"Billy ready. Though I should also say," added Billy in an undertone, "that we are, without doubt, gonna d-i-i-ie."

"Not today," said Mary decisively. "We're going to finish this, once and for all. We're right at the heart of the Alliance of Evil. These Rogues have been menacing us like a . . . like a mean snake. And you know the best way to deal with a snake? Cut off its head."

"I think I'd be more inclined to run away, going *'Aaaargh, snake!'*" said Billy reasonably. But he ballooned a hand in readiness for combat.

"Angel ready!" came a bright, enthusiastic voice from behind them.

"Ah yes," said Mary. "Angel. About that. Stay here with the *Banshee* and keep her prepped."

"No way!" exclaimed Angel. "I'm coming with you! Let's turn and burn!"

"Again, I have no idea what that means," Mary replied. "Listen, I know you want action, but I need you to be our lookout. If we can, we're going to rescue Murph and get out of here. But if anything goes wrong . . ."

"Something will definitely go wrong," added Billy.

". . . you need to contact the Alliance," finished Mary. "And if necessary, you need to go and fetch help. You know how to fly the *Banshee*. Plus there's no way I'm taking you in there to face Magpie again. Your mom would quite literally kill me."

"Fine," said Angel steadily, flopping down into the pilot's chair and smiling ruefully. "I'll wait. Just this once. **And only because I respect you, Canary."**

"Thank you. The rest of you, we don't know what we'll be faced with or what state of mind Murph will be in," said Mary, "so stay as calm as possible. Billy, I'm looking at you."

The most unconvincing smile ever appeared on Billy's face.

"We need to be cautious. If this is a rescue mission, then great. But we don't know what hold Magpie has over Murph, or if it'll be safe to make the attempt. If that's not the case, let's get as much information as possible, so we can report back to Jasper. **Keep your wits about you,"** Mary told her team, leading them down the brick passageway and toward that unearthly purple light.

"So . . . I came," Murph Cooper told Magpie simply. "What do you want?"

"I told you, I want to give you a gift," replied the man in black. "One that will help you greatly. I'm going to give you one of my superpowers."

Murph's mind reeled. He hadn't been expecting that. "What do you mean?" he asked warily.

"I know what it's like to be an outcast, you see,"

said Magpie, turning away from Murph and beginning to pace back and forth. "I understand what these past few weeks must have been like for you. Spurned and rejected by your friends as you secretly plotted against them. As soon as your . . . missions"— he curled his lip sarcastically—"started to go wrong, there was nobody who truly stood by you. They saw you as an encumbrance. A nuisance. A stupid kid with no power of his own, who relies on his more capable friends to rescue him, time and time and time again."

Murph was feeling more and more uncomfortable. He understood perfectly well that Magpie didn't really want to help him. He knew that the man in black was a sworn enemy of the Heroes' Alliance and all it stood for. But he was at such a low ebb, so drained of hope, that some of Magpie's words were starting to take hold in his mind.

"Trust me, Kid Normal, they have never accepted you as one of their own," continued Magpie. "Not truly. And they realized, didn't they, in the end? Realized that they'd be better off without you?"

Murph dropped his head. He could think of no response.

"Don't worry," soothed Magpie. "I understand. And I can help you. Because I think you've finally realized what your Heroes' Alliance has known all along . . . That being Kid Normal isn't really all that special after all."

Murph struggled to lift his mind out of the murk of misery that Magpie's words were heaping on top of him. His friends *had* blamed him . . . they *did* think he was useless . . . the Heroes' Alliance *had* rejected him. Kid Normal was finished.

"The Shadow Machine can change all that," said Magpie gently, gesturing toward the flattened metal pyramid with its two glowing orbs. "All you have to do is take a deep breath and climb those steps to the top. It will be worth it, now that you are ready to receive the great gift I'm offering. Now that you know you are truly alone."

"Oh no he isn't!" rang out a voice from the doorway.

*

"What happened to 'We need to be cautious'?" Mary asked Hilda curtly as the Super Zeroes lined up in the archway. They had managed to approach secretly—it seemed that Magpie had been too caught up in his speech to use his super-hearing to listen for them coming—but Hilda's shout of "Oh no he isn't!" had somewhat given the game away.

"I just got so annoyed with Magpie," fumed Hilda. "Telling Murph that he's all alone and he isn't special! **I just won't tolerate that!**" She stamped her foot.

Murph had turned to face his friends in confusion. "What are you doing here?" he asked, looking horrified.

Mary was flabbergasted. "Rescuing you, of course. What did you think?" she sputtered. But there was no time for Murph to reply. Magpie pushed him roughly to one side as he stalked up to the Super Zeroes.

"Oh dear, dear, dear," he said mock-sadly. "Were we hoping to write a lovely little adventure story? The one where the nice, daring children track the baddie down to his lair? The one where they defeat him, against all the odds? The one where they rescue their little friend?" He chuckled—a dry, rasping sound like a croaking bird. "I think we've all read that story before, haven't we? And you know what? I think it's gotten a bit BORING!" He shouted this last word shockingly loudly. The echoes snickered at them from the walls and the glass-domed ceiling.

Now Magpie turned on Murph, who still seemed dumbstruck.

"Don't think that because your friends have followed you here they see you as their equal. This is merely more proof that loyalty and teamwork are nothing but a pathetic fable," Magpie hissed. "Your friends should be safe at home with their mommies and daddies. Instead, they walk right into the lion's den! All because they think you can't take care of yourself!"

Guilt stabbed at Mary. **"Don't listen to him, Murph, that's not what this is,"** she said.

"It's going to make for a lovely surprise twist to the end of this tale, though," mocked Magpie. "A doomed last stand to save the leader they rejected."

"Nobody's rejected anybody," Mary was almost yelling now. "And nobody's doomed, either. We got the best of you before, Magpie, and we'll do it again!"

"We'll thwart you as many times as we have to," shouted Hilda, pushing back her sleeves, dropping into a combat stance, and popping her horses into existence.

"Unless you want to give in now and save yourself the bother," snarled Billy, gesturing at the horses. With a sound like a horse-shaped novelty balloon being rapidly inflated, they expanded into two massive snorting, rearing stallions.

"Yes, if you come quietly, we can just show you back to a nice quiet cell where you won't bother anyone," added Mary, extending her umbrella and preparing to fly into combat.

Nellie was too enraged to speak, but she looked at Magpie with cold fury. The clouds already bulging above them in the darkening sky began to boil and thicken, and a low drum-roll of thunder echoed from the rocky hills.

Magpie looked from face to face impassively. Then he dropped his head.

For a split second Mary actually thought he was about to submit, but then she heard a chilling sound. Magpie's shoulders heaved, and a twisted chuckle escaped from between his thin lips. He reached up a hand and wiped his eyes. "How wonderful!" He laughed. "You must have known how it would end."

"Get him!" Mary yelled, running forward. She knew they couldn't afford to give Magpie time to strike. But a split second was all it took.

Magpie let out a gloating, high-pitched shriek, throwing his arms to the sky and summoning huge crackling bolts of purple lightning that wound around the four Super Zeroes, trapping them inside a glowing cage. He jerked his arms downward, firing yet more bolts of energy. The first of them hit Billy, and he cried out in pain and confusion, dropping to his knees and clutching his head in his hands. The horses shrank back to their usual size.

"NO!" cried Hilda. **"Please! Please!"** Magpie looked at her without an ounce of pity, curling his face into a cruel leer and gesturing at her with a finger. A beam of energy knocked her backward, and her horses vanished.

Sheets of lightning flashed in the clouds above as Nellie's fury prepared to break, but she never got the time. Another burst of purple fire from Magpie's hands enveloped her, and she too slumped to the floor.

Mary made a final, desperate attempt to cut Magpie off by diving to one side, popping her umbrella open and soaring into the air. She avoided the onslaught of purple energy bolts by jerking from side to side like a kite in a storm. She shut her mind off to what had happened to her friends—it was too enormous and too horrific to contemplate.

But she could only dodge Magpie's Cape-stealing energy for so long. She thought she heard Murph give a desperate shout—**"DON'T!"**—but almost at the same moment, one of the bolts struck her. Her head swam and the scene in front of her blurred. She felt as if the very life force was being sucked out of her—transmitted back down the purple lightning bolt to infuse Magpie's bent, twisted body. Then she felt herself tumbling head over heels to the ground and braced for a shattering impact. But just before she came to earth, she felt arms around her and a soft body below. Nellie had thrown herself at the floor to break her friend's fall.

"This is where teamwork gets you, Kid Normal!" roared Magpie. "You led your friends into danger. You have no power—you had nothing to lose. But to save you, they gambled everything. They gambled it, and lost."

He turned to face the rest of the Super Zeroes. They were huddling together under the onslaught of scorn.

"I hope you are all happy with the leader you chose. Be thankful you still have your lives."

He gestured with his hands, and the metal floor around them began to warp and ripple like a restless sea. Mary, Nellie, Hilda, and Billy—still shell-shocked from having their Capes stolen—were moved by some invisible force to the corner of the large room. The floor rose up around them to encase them inside thick walls as Magpie's powers conjured an impenetrable cell out of nowhere. A thick, riveted door with a barred window completed their prison. Mary knew better than to see if it was unlocked.

"Thanks for the powers," sneered Magpie once the four were securely shut away. He shut his eyes and licked his thin lips, as if savoring the unique flavor of each Cape. "I've never felt a storm-summoning power as potent as this one. Delicious. I don't think the ponies will be very useful, though." He jerked his hands forward, and two misshapen, sickly-looking horses appeared—a pale mockery of Hilda's own, snarling and snapping at each other.

Hilda let out a strangled sob.

"Now that really is a pointless power, isn't it?" mused Magpie, snapping the horses back out of existence again and stalking toward the stairs that led to the top of the metal pyramid.

Mary looked around at her friends inside the cell. Hilda had buried her head in her hands. Billy was lying on the floor, ashen-faced. Nellie came over and hugged Mary, silent tears streaming down her face and splashing off her friend's yellow raincoat.

They were beaten.

This was the end.

A LETTER FROM THE AUTHORS

Dear Sir or Madam reading this book,

In our previous works, we have been known to insert a story about a rabbit into the narrative at times of high tension like the one you just experienced.

We would like to apologize unreservedly to all our readers for this course of action. Breaking into a dramatic superhero story with a ridiculous tale about a rabbit who goes on amazing adventures is both patronizing and childish.

We would like to reassure you that when you turn the page, you will find a continuation of *Kid Normal and the Shadow Machine*.

Not a story about Alan Rabbit.

Nope.

Nuh-uh.

No siree.

That would just be silly.

Yours in serious literature,

Gregopher and Christory

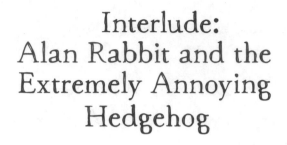

Interlude:
Alan Rabbit and the Extremely Annoying Hedgehog

Once upon a time there were three little bunny rabbits, and their names were Dandelion, Flopperty, and Alan. They lived in a large semidetached rabbit hole with their mother, who was a bus driver.

One fine spring day, when Mrs. Pollyanna Rabbit had left to drive an amateur rabbit mixed martial arts team to a regional competition, the three children opened the door of their burrow and sniffed the air.

It was a beautiful morning. The sun shone, cows were doing lunges, and in a nearby treetop

a quartet of
larks was performing a
close-harmony version of "Circle
of Life."

"I shall gather berries from the
hedgerow to make supper," declared
Dandelion, who was a good little
rabbit, if slightly smug and annoying.

"I shall hop around in circles barking
like a dog," decided Flopperty, who had
issues.

"I shall go exploring in Mr. McDougal's
garden, even though nobody has ever
come out of there alive, including
my own father," said Alan, who was
a fool.

So Alan Rabbit, who was
wearing a blue jacket in spite of
the fact that his species had evolved
a dense furry coat of its own over
countless millions of

years, scampered straight
away to Mr. McDougal's garden
and squeezed under the fence, just
beside a large sign that read:

NO RABBITS to enter here on pain of death.
Seriously. You will not come out alive. I have
several guns. It's not worth it. There is plenty
of free food available: you literally eat grass.
There is no need to come into my garden and
attempt to steal human food. I WILL kill you.
Love, Mr. McDougal.

Alan flolloped around the flower
beds. First he ate some string. Then
he ate some gravel. And then, feeling
rather sick, he went to look for
some aspirin.

As he rounded a corner, he came across a very peculiar person.

She had on an apron and a white cloth cap, and she was carrying a basket of washing. But sticking out from her cap and all down her back were rows and rows of sharp prickles.

"Good morning, if you please, ma'am," said the stranger in an unnecessarily loud voice. "My name, if you please, ma'am, is Mrs.—" and she let out a loud shriek like a bird—"KAAAAARK!"

"Sorry," said Alan. "Your name is . . . what?"

"Mrs. KAAAAAAAAAAAARK!" screamed the little person. From the other side of the garden there came a soft clicking as Mr. McDougal loaded his very largest gun.

"Can we keep

the noise down a bit, Mrs., um . . . Kark?" pleaded Alan.

"No, it's louder than that," she corrected him, "and more high-pitched. Sort of like this . . . KAAAAAAAARRRRRRRKKKKK!!!"

"Okay, okay, got it," said Alan Rabbit, desperately shushing her.

"I'm a little old washerwoman, ma'am," said Mrs. KAAAAAARRK proudly.

"You are quite clearly a hedgehog," corrected Alan Rabbit. "And a nutcase. And stop calling me 'ma'am.'"

"I'm an excellent clear-starcher," gibbered the hedgehog. "I can starch your pocket handkins." And she sang him the following song, which you must once again make up your own tune for and sing as loudly as you can, preferably in the kitchen.

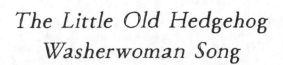

The Little Old Hedgehog
Washerwoman Song

Scrubbly bubbly, prickly pickers,
I am a hedgehog who washes your knickers.
Lovely scrubbly, prickly peas,
Even though I am infested with fleas.

Oh, squirrels are policemen,
And voles they mend the roads,
Larks are all accountants,
And the lawyers, they are toads.
Mayflies work as pastry chefs,
And each lamb is a vet.
But every little hedgehog,
Works inside a launderette.

Scrubbly bubbly, prickly pickers,
I am a hedgehog who washes your knickers.
Lovely scrubbly, prickly peas,
Even though I am infested with fleas.

"Seriously, shut up," scolded Alan. But it was too late. There was a crunching of huge boots on the gravel path, and Mr. McDougal appeared at the end of a bed of geraniums. He was wearing sunglasses, wielding an enormous machine gun, and walking in slow motion.

"HASTA LA VISTA, BABY," snarled Mr. McDougal in his deep, Austrian accent, preparing to fire.

But before he could unleash his attack, there was a strange whooshing noise. A small blue telephone booth appeared near Alan Rabbit, and the door opened.

"Come with me if you want to live," said a voice from inside. Alan looked in to see a grizzled old rabbit wearing a long scarf beckoning to him urgently.

"What's the blue box all about?" asked Alan, who was a millennial rabbit and had never used a telephone booth.

"There's no time to explain," said the old rabbit.

"There totally is," argued Alan. "You could have explained briefly in the few seconds it took you to say 'There's no time to explain' just then."

"Would you like me to iron lovely creases into your pantaloons?" asked the hedgehog, brandishing a clothes press.

"Jump!" shouted the grizzled old rabbit in the phone booth.

"BANG!" added Mr. McDougal's machine gun.

Oh well, thought Alan Rabbit to himself. *This day literally could not get any weirder.* And he leaped into the air and sailed through the door of the blue telephone booth.

"Thanks for the save," he told the old rabbit as the box dematerialized.

"You're welcome," the old rabbit told him, pulling a stick of celery out of his top pocket and using it to clean out one of his ears. There was a squelching, popping sound as he removed the celery from his ear, and then another one as the phone booth rematerialized.

"We are now millions of years in the past," said the time-traveling rabbit, hopping to the door and opening it. "Look—dinosaurs! And they seem hungry!"

"Well, isn't that just great," said Alan Rabbit sarcastically.

ANOTHER LETTER FROM THE AUTHORS

We would like to apologize for the previous letter from the authors, which appeared at the end of the preceding chapter.

In that letter, we promised that the narrative would not be interrupted by a story about a rabbit. And yet, the aforementioned letter was followed immediately by an interlude entitled "Alan Rabbit and the Extremely Annoying Hedgehog."

We want to apologize unreservedly for breaking our promise to continue with the story without interruption. Furthermore, we would like to apologize for following the rabbit story—which, we acknowledge, was childish and tiresome—with a further interruption, i.e. this letter, which is, if anything, even more childish and annoying.

The story shall now proceed forthwith, henceforth, and without delay.

Sorry again.

Seriously. Sorry.

On with the story!

Love,

Gres and Chrig

16

The Hall of Lost Heroes

Mary's entire body ached, and she felt sick and weak. With a huge effort, she dragged herself to her feet and pressed her face to the bars on their cell door. She could see Magpie standing at the base of the Shadow Machine. The man in black caught her eye briefly as he flexed his knees. With a horrified thrill, she realized what he was about to do.

Magpie launched himself skyward, soaring like a tattered scrap of ash borne up from a bonfire, landing neatly on the platform on top of his machine. Seeing him use her Cape made Mary's head swim with dismay, but she bit her lip and told herself to keep focused. She couldn't let Magpie get inside her mind.

Murph was standing not far away, with his back to her and his head bowed, at the foot of the metal staircase.

"Murph!" she hissed at him. "Murph! Whatever he's made you do, it's okay! **We can sort this out! Just . . . don't give in!"**

Murph turned to her, his face haunted. "You lost your Capes because you followed me!" he said in a broken voice. "How can anything ever be okay . . . ever again? You don't know what I've done. If you did you wouldn't have come."

"I know it was you sabotaging our missions!" Mary started to say, "and I don't care! I—"

But she was interrupted by a cry of "Activate!" Magpie had lifted his arms and gestured toward the ceiling. Craning her neck through the bars, Mary saw a set of blinking purple lights illuminate a series of cameras arranged around the enormous room.

"Good evening, fools of the Heroes' Alliance," the man in black was saying in a loud, self-satisfied voice. "This is Magpie. I trust I have your attention."

Mary realized he must be broadcasting across the HALO network. With a chill, she imagined the members of the Alliance watching what was going on—in

318

Witchberry Hall, in countless vehicles, on the wrists of Heroes—even on the control panel of the *Banshee* next door.

"I have something to share with you all," Magpie continued, spinning around and throwing his arms wide. "About the childish . . . *fable* you have built up around this boy. This . . . Kid Normal." Mary heard the cameras whine as they turned to point at Murph, still standing glumly and silently at the base of the Shadow Machine.

"You looked up to this young Hero," Magpie went on. "You thought of him as a great example, a shining beacon of how your Alliance can move forward." He stared down at Murph and beckoned for him to climb the stairs. "The reality is rather different."

Mary watched in disbelief as Murph obediently began to climb to the top of the Shadow Machine as Magpie went on. "For weeks now he has been working for me! He has sabotaged his team's missions, allowing my associates in the Alliance of Evil to continue their work. He has led his friends here tonight and allowed me to steal their Capabilities! And now—" he licked his thin lips—"the legend of Kid Normal is about to die, once and for all."

Murph had reached the top of the steps.

"You all revered him because he led a team of Heroes without one of your precious Capabilities. Without ever feeling the lack of one, or wishing he was different. It gave you all hope that, no matter what odds were stacked against you, the good guys could prevail. That anyone could find the strength to be a Hero," Magpie said. "But I am about to show you that that, too, is a lie. I have constructed the greatest piece of mind-sharing technology the world has ever seen—the Shadow Machine. It has the power to transfer one of my own Capabilities to young Mr. Cooper here. And see how eagerly he leaps at the chance! The moment he is given the opportunity to gain a power—he takes it! So you see, there was nothing really so very admirable about Kid Normal after all."

Magpie spun around, as if looking around at the faces of his massive, unseen audience. Then he moved to one of the two glowing purple orbs on top of the platform and turned his attention to Murph.

"When you place your hands on the other orb,

Kid Normal," he said, "our minds will be linked. You will be able to pick one of my stolen powers as your own. And then your journey will be complete." He took a deep breath and placed his palms on the orb.

Immediately the Shadow Machine clanked into life. The large wheels and gears inside the pyramid began to spin faster. Sparks and flashing lights ran along the wires and pipes, and jets of steam hissed off into the night air. The purple light coming from the orbs gradually grew brighter and brighter until Magpie was hardly visible. "Join me, Kid Normal!" he was shouting. "Enter the Shadow Machine!"

Hilda had managed to get to her feet and was peering through the bars behind Mary. "He's not going to do it, is he?" she asked her, horrified. "Murph would never let Magpie manipulate him like that . . . would he?"

"I never thought he would . . ." Mary said. "There's got to be more to this. There has to be something we're not seeing . . ."

But as she watched, Murph Cooper stepped forward and placed his own hands firmly on the second orb.

As Murph put his hands on the orb, it was as if the world had been turned off like a TV set. All he could see in front of him was Magpie, standing in the middle of a bright white fog. He could hear nothing but his own breathing—no clanking from the machine and no shouting from Mary. Just him and his breaths, which were growing faster and shallower. He felt cut off from everything else in the universe.

Like he had stepped into a dream.

Gradually, shadowy figures appeared in the fog—and these quickly solidified until he found himself among a horde of solid shadow shapes almost like a gallery of wax statues.

He found that he was able to move among the shadows like a visitor at a museum. Tall figures and short, stooped ones, frozen in time while running, fighting, or striking heroic poses—they stretched away into the distance.

High above his head, Murph could see blurry, disjointed images flashing in the fog, as if a projector was casting snatches of different films. He walked forward, and as he moved closer to one of the black statues, ones of these images came into focus.

The image was of the inside of Magpie's cell in Shivering Sands. It felt as if he was standing at the bottom of the stone steps, looking upward as purple jets of lightning shot from his outstretched hands.

Memories, he thought to himself. *I'm seeing Magpie's memories.* He turned away from the image to look back down at the shadow figure in front of him and realized with a shock that it was Miss Flint.

"Murph the ice monster. Yes, that's a thought," came Magpie's voice, though he couldn't now see where the man in black was—the voice seemed to come from everywhere. "Simply step into the shadow before you, and that superpower will be transferred to you. I think you'll make an excellent Rogue, you know. You'll soon realize the true meaning of power—it means not needing anyone else. Then you'll be truly great. Who knows? You might even be a match for me!" His laugh echoed around the space.

Murph instinctively recoiled from the shadow of Miss Flint as the full realization of where he was hit home.

This is Magpie's mind, he told himself, looking around in renewed horror at the palace of powers that surrounded him. *I'm inside his mind, with his stolen Capes all around me.*

"Are you now realizing the true wonder of the Shadow Machine?" said the voice of Magpie. "Yes, it's really quite impressive, isn't it? Take a look around, Kid Normal. Although we'll have to think of another name for you soon, won't we? You're not going to stay normal for very much longer. Not now that you understand what I'm offering you."

Murph moved through the motionless Hero shadows, his own mind racing. He'd have to pick something, he realized. Magpie had backed him into a corner. Not for himself—even with a Cape, he knew the Heroes' Alliance wouldn't have him back. But was there a power that would allow him to rescue his mom and Andy? He wondered. Could he keep Magpie busy long enough to let them escape, at least?

"All my powers are ranged before you," the disembodied voice was saying. "And you may pick any of them."

All your powers? thought Murph, curious. Something about that phrase had caused the beginnings of an idea to swirl around his brain. *All of them? Every single one?* He felt a tiny flaring of warmth in his chest and his breathing slowed. *Is it just possible? Is there actually a way to end this once and for all?*

"Of course," Magpie went on, "power can be a lonely business. But you know that now, don't you? You realize that your so-called friends were only a convenience. A defense mechanism. When you have an ability of your own, you'll understand properly."

With a sharp pang, Murph saw four figures lined up in front of him. They were unmistakable, even without the umbrella one of them was holding.

"Ah, yes," mused Magpie's voice. "I wondered if perhaps you might choose one of their powers."

In the sky above, Magpie's memory of a few minutes ago flashed into view. Murph saw his four friends, ready to fight to the end to save him. Murph looked at the expression on Mary's face as she flew into the air—determined and confident—and suddenly he knew that the pilot light inside him was still burning. The

Heroes' Alliance might have thrown him out. They might be watching now, convinced that he had gone power-crazy. But he had just worked out how he could win.

The audacity of the plan took his breath away, but it was the only way. He had to take the fight to Magpie. For too long now, the battle had been on someone else's terms. Kid Normal was about to take the initiative.

Moving with more purpose, Murph walked through the hall of shadow statues. As he passed each of them, flashes of the moments Magpie had stolen this or that Cape flashed in the fog above him. But he barely stopped to look. He knew now exactly which power he was searching for.

Gradually the figures began to thin out. And as they did so, Murph began to feel a resistance, as if an invisible force was trying to push him back. Inwardly he smiled. Magpie was beginning to realize that he might have made a critical mistake.

"Invisibility? Is that what you are searching for?" came the Rogue's voice, from everywhere and yet nowhere. "Your friend the Blue Phantom would want you to have that, I'm sure. Or flight? Laser beams? Make your choice . . . come on . . ."

Magpie sounded calm, but Murph thought he detected a faint, fluttering edge of anxiety in that last sentence. A hint of desperation. Murph knew that once he had showed his hand he was going to have to move extremely fast, and he clenched his fists and set his jaw in readiness.

As he continued to walk forward, the force trying to hold him back became stronger. Before long it was like trying to wade through oatmeal. Now the figures surrounding him were only thinly spaced, and the white mist was growing thicker, almost obscuring some of them.

"The best powers are behind you," wheedled Magpie's voice, the desperation now showing. But Murph carried on. He knew just what he was looking for—and before long he saw it.

Near the far corner of the enormous space, just where the mist seemed to thicken into walls and curve upward, was the figure of a man with upraised swords for hands. Murph remembered the story he had been told by Sir Jasper Rowntree earlier that year.

"The Dandy Man," he said out loud. "The first Hero you ever stole a power from."

"And a singularly useless power at that," said Magpie uneasily. "I have hardly used that laughable ability since—Why should it concern you?"

The memory of that long-ago day was playing above Murph's head. Jerky and washed-out like an old movie, the Dandy Man, in his ridiculous highwayman's hat swishing his swords, looked just as Jasper had described to Murph when they'd first met.

"The Dandy Man's Cape doesn't concern me," said Kid Normal, smiling slightly. "I'm more concerned with what's behind it."

"That was my first theft . . ." replied Magpie, even more hesitantly. "There is nothing more."

Murph stepped around the statue of the Dandy Man, right to the very corner of the room of mist. Right to the hidden heart of the Shadow Machine. Right to the one power that Magpie had hoped he would not realize was there. Because, unlike most of the Heroes in this hall of statues, it was not an impressive figure. It was small and stooped, and almost hidden in the mist. If you were looking for a superpower, it was a figure you would overlook.

There, in the corner, stood the figure of a young boy about Murph's age. It was hard to tell from the shadowy silhouette, indistinct as it was in the swirling mist, but it seemed to be cowering or cringing downward almost as if fending off a blow. As Murph approached it—with great difficulty—and as the invisible force tried desperately to hold him back, a different set of memories began to flash above his head.

They were sepia toned and out of focus, as if they came from very, very long ago. And this time, there was sound—tinny and faint—accompanying them.

"Stealing again . . ." someone was shouting. A frightening-looking man in old-fashioned clothes lifted an arm.

"Go on, get out of here! Nobody wants you!" A sea of younger faces was visible now, looking threatening and fierce.

"You've got no friends!"
"You're nothing!"

"I thought so," said Murph, kindly and a little sadly. "You're all the same, at the end of the day, you Rogues. Somewhere along the line you get a twisted idea of what power can do for you. But by the time you work out that it can't get you love, or friendship, or even happiness, it's too late, isn't it? Magpie, I've made my

choice. I don't need any of the powers you've stolen.

I just need the one you've always had."

"NO!" screamed Magpie's voice. "Get out of my head! GET OUT OF MY MACHINE!"

"It's not your machine any more," said Kid Normal calmly. **"It's mine."**

And he stepped into the final shadow.

17

The Master of
the Shadow Machine

Mary, of course, had seen none of this, and neither had the watching members of the Heroes' Alliance. She gripped the bars of their cell, peering into the white mist, but all she could see were the figures of Murph and Magpie standing motionless and silent with their hands fixed to those purple orbs.

"What's going on?" Hilda wondered aloud. **"What are they doing up there?"**

For several long minutes the two figures stood like statues as the wheels of the Shadow Machine clanked and whirred beneath them, visible through the iron mesh. Then the pitch of the machine changed. The gears started to whine, and steam began to pour out of the metal pyramid. The mist on top began to whirl around and around, and a bright white light surrounded the two frozen silhouettes.

"Oh no, this is it," said Hilda solemnly. "Come on, Murph, resist!"

"I can't look!" cried Billy, who had also joined them. Mary put an arm around him.

"Come on, Murph," urged Mary under her breath. "This isn't you. You know it isn't."

Suddenly the light around Magpie changed color, from bright white to a dark, rich purple. Like water being drained from a tall, thin glass, this purple light sank into the orb through Magpie's hand—and at the same time, that same color purple appeared on Murph's side of the machine, growing out of his orb to suffuse his whole body with a bright, crackling light. The white mist whipped itself into a whirlwind that was sucked down into the heart of the device, and vanished. And then, just as the sound of the machine and the intensity of the light were building to an unbearable scream, everything stopped.

Murph and Magpie were facing each other across the metal platform, like a pair of sleepers who had just awoken. Mary could see Murph shake his head, as if trying to clear his thoughts. Then, suddenly, he threw himself sideways and pelted desperately down the metal stairs toward her. Magpie, with an animallike bellow of pure fury, fired bolts of energy after him, but they slammed harmlessly into the walls of their cell.

"I've taken it!" panted Murph to her as he ran toward them. **"I've taken his Cape!"**

"Which one?" shouted Mary in confusion.

"His own one! The first one!" yelled Murph as he ran off. "The main one! No time to explain! Got a plan! But please tell me you brought Angel with you!"

"We did. She's back where you left the *Wyvern*," Mary shouted.

"What does he mean, he's taken Magpie's power?" said Hilda, confused. "Does this mean he isn't Kid Normal anymore?"

"He's gone power mad," decided Billy mournfully.

"Why does he want Angel? This is odd," whispered Nellie, shaking her hair over her face and sitting down on the floor in one corner.

"No!" Mary replied. "He says he's got a plan—and he wants—"

"ANGEL!" Murph was bellowing, as he dodged another volley of lightning bolts from Magpie. The man in black was still at the top of the Shadow Machine—Mary could see him looking around desperately for his enemy through the smoke and steam.

Her mind was in turmoil. Had Murph really wanted to take Magpie's power? The thing that had made him the most feared enemy the world of Heroes had ever known? What on earth was going through his mind? She hoped against hope that he hadn't truly listened to Magpie's lies about powers and teamwork, but there was no way to be entirely sure. It had been a very strange half an hour for everyone involved.

As Murph darted past the metal prison that held his friends, he noticed that Magpie had gone disconcertingly quiet.

He'll be planning a counterattack, he thought. Magpie was now on the defensive—and Murph knew from wildlife documentaries that a cornered predator is the most dangerous animal of all. He also knew that otters mate for life, that slugs have four noses, and that wombat poo is cube-shaped, but only one of these four animal facts was relevant at this exact moment in time.

He steeled himself and picked up the pace. He was going to need excellent timing, and a great deal of luck, to carry off his extremely daring and pretty much made-up-on-the-spur-of-the-moment plan to defeat Magpie once and for all. There would be no time to test out his new power—the first time he used it in anger it would have to work just as he needed.

He was also wrestling with a very strange sensation: the knowledge that he suddenly had the ability to collect as many superpowers as he wanted. For now, at least, he was no longer Kid Normal. He was Kid Exceptional. Kid Powerful. Kid Dangerous. It was a heady and uncomfortable feeling. *I understand how this could drive you a bit crazy*, he thought.

"ANGEL!" he bellowed again.

Luckily Angel, who'd been watching these events unfold on the *Banshee*'s HALO screen, had already decided that she'd stayed out of harm's way long enough.

There was a roar from the brick tunnel that connected the huge concrete chimney with the Shadow Machine control room, and Murph saw a bright headlight approaching through the dust and smoke. With a lick of flame from its twin exhausts, the *Wyvern* burst out of the tunnel and skidded to a halt beside him, Angel at the controls.

"Did somebody call for backup?" she shouted over the engine's roar and the explosions that were still firing off all around them as Magpie desperately tried to keep his quarry at bay.

Murph climbed up behind her. "I certainly did," he told her. "Now listen. Some pretty weird stuff is about to go down. I need you to get me close to Magpie—I'm going to steal some of his Capes."

"What? Steal . . . his Capes? But how . . . ?"

"There isn't time to explain!" he yelled. "You're going to have to trust me! Just do as I say! Between us we can make all this right again, I promise! Let's move!"

Angel gunned the motorcycle, thumbing switches

on the control
panel with her
left hand. **"You got
it, Cooper,"** she shouted to him. **"Hang on!"**

The rear wheel of the bike kicked up a plume of
brick dust from the floor as the engine roared, then
the *Wyvern* shot into the air and began to circle the
Shadow Machine as Magpie spun around, desperately
trying to follow it. He raised his arms to fire a fresh
fusillade of energy bolts.

"Next pass," Murph screamed into Angel's
ear. **"Get as close as you can!"**

Angel eased the handlebars to the left, and the
motorcycle swooped down toward the machine. Murph
could clearly see the twin orbs, still glowing with a faint
purple light, but focused all his attention on Magpie.

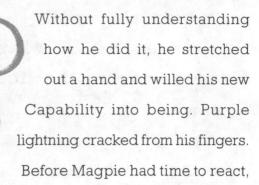

Without fully understanding how he did it, he stretched out a hand and willed his new Capability into being. Purple lightning cracked from his fingers. Before Magpie had time to react, he was surrounded by it, and he cried out in pain as his energy bolts abruptly stopped firing.

Murph felt as if his whole body was being pumped full of energy—it was a feeling he was never able to forget for the rest of his life—stealing a power for the first time.

"All right," he told Angel. "Get ready! This one's for you!" Concentrating, he fired off his own burst of energy bolts at the platform. "Can you mirror that?" he asked her.

"Got it!" she replied.

"Open the cell!" he told her, and then, raising his voice to a shout, **"Mary! All of you! Get away from the door!"**

Angel unleashed a stream of energy bolts at the cell door just as Mary heeded Murph's warning and dragged the others back. Angel's magnified bolts ripped the door from its hinges and fired it across the huge room like a Frisbee. It **panged** into the far wall in a burst of sparks.

Magpie, still on top of the Shadow Machine, had sunk to his knees—for the first time in his long life learning how it felt to have a Capability stolen away from him. Murph knew he had to act before the Rogue had time to rally.

"Can you land us on there?" he asked Angel.

"Easy," she replied, steering the bike downward. "Hold on!"

Mary, Billy, Nellie, and Hilda stepped gingerly out of their cell, braced for combat even without their Capes.

"Mary! Hello! Help!" a voice was shouting from somewhere above.

Mary looked up and saw Murph's mom waving an

arm through the barred window of a cell on the platform. The final piece of the jigsaw slotted neatly into place.

"Murph's mom! Of course!" Suddenly she understood. *"That's* how he forced Murph to work with him. Blackmail! I *hate* blackmail. It's the absolute worst. Come on!" The Super Zeroes raced for the spiral staircase.

The *Wyvern*, meanwhile, had made a rough landing on top of the machine, turning on its side and skidding across the metal platform with Murph and Angel tumbling off as it went. Once again Murph concentrated, in preparation for stealing a Capability from the man in black, who was stumbling to his feet, disorientated from the last attack.

This time Murph knew exactly what he was aiming for. He needed the power that had built this machine in the first place.

"Okay, Angel. This is it," declared Murph. "I'm going to grab his tele-tech."

"What's it like being Magpie, Cooper?" she asked.

Murph laughed at the question.

"Pretty stressful, to be quite honest with you. And my entire body aches! But it'll be over soon. All right, let's both concentrate. I'm going to need you to mirror this when we get in position." He urgently whispered his plan into Angel's ear. "Up for it?" he finished.

"Of course, Captain Cooper! I'm with you!" she replied.

The rest of the Zeroes paused on the platform as Murph and Angel crouched at the edge. Murph tried to blot out the noise and the smell of the battle all around him and focus. He just desperately hoped that this machine could do what he hoped it could. *Surely*, he thought to himself, *if it can transfer a Cape from one person to another . . . it can do this.* There was only one way to find out. He needed tele-tech. The power that Magpie had stolen from Sir Jasper Rowntree all those years ago. The power to alter electronics and machinery with his mind.

But Magpie wasn't defeated yet. He still had plenty of Capabilities—and, driven to the brink of madness by his near-defeat, he was prepared to fight with all the rage and callousness at his disposal. He finally lurched to his feet, hands locked like claws, and suddenly Angel was lifted off her feet by an invisible force field and thrown like a rag doll from the platform. She hit the ground and rolled out of the way as Magpie aimed a huge jet of fire at her.

Up on the platform, Nellie and Billy were struggling with the lock on the cell door. An electronic number pad was beside it, and Billy was frantically punching numbers in.

"Anyone know Magpie's date of birth?" he asked desperately.

Down on the Shadow Machine, Murph hit Magpie with more bursts of purple lightning, not even caring for the moment what powers he stole. He just needed to slow him down. But even in the midst of the battle, he felt a jolt of pure joy when he realized his feet had lifted off the metal platform. *I can fly*, he thought to himself. *I got Mary's Cape. I can fly.*

Dodging another jet of flame from Magpie, he soared down to the ground and landed—not especially neatly— next to Angel. "We need to get back up there," he told her. **"And if I can fly, so can you."**

"Yup," she confirmed. "After all, I'm only as good as the Hero I'm standing next to."

"Aren't we all?" said Kid Normal. And together, they floated back up to the top of the Shadow Machine. Murph instantly knocked Magpie to his knees with another web of purple lightning, and as another new power was sucked into his body, his eyes lit up with triumph. This was the one he needed—he could feel it.

As the tele-tech suffused him, Murph was suddenly aware of the myriad of electronic systems and connections that made up the machine below him. He marveled at the mind that had put it all together. But he also knew, instinctively, that the machine was capable of changing. It could be altered to do his bidding.

"Quick, Angel, before he recovers!" he yelled. **"Just like I told you! Now!"**

His face bright red and sweating with the effort, Kid Normal unleashed his latest Cape. He sent his tele-tech down into the Shadow Machine, willing it to change. And almost immediately he felt another power join his own, as Angel brought her own will to bear.

Together, Murph and the girl he'd saved after thirty years of imprisonment stood together, eyes closed, heads bowed, and gave the Shadow Machine their instructions.

Magpie screeched like some monstrous, furious bird, preparing to unleash the sum total of all his remaining Capabilities in one desperate, final attack. If it had succeeded, it would have completely destroyed all three of them. And anyone else nearby for that matter.

But the attack never came.

Because, as Magpie lifted his hands, balling crackling purple electricity in preparation to strike . . .

And as Mary, Nellie, Billy, and Hilda looked on in fear and awe from the iron platform . . .

And as the Heroes' Alliance looked in wonder at their HALO screens . . .

Kid Normal activated his machine.

18

Stolen Goods

There was a hideous grinding, creaking noise as Kid Normal's reconfigured Shadow Machine came to life. It was as if the very heart of the device was protesting at its new role. Wheels and gears shrieked in protest—emitting a huge scraping, discordant din as they spun and rearranged. It sounded as if the whole machine was screaming in pain and total fury. The entire Titan Thirteen power plant began to shake to its foundations.

The Zeroes grabbed on to the bars of the platform up above for stability.

"The whole place is going to collapse!" screeched Billy in panic, and although he'd never considered a career as an opera singer, he actually hit a perfect High C with the final syllable. Nellie scrambled over to him across the rocking floor and held his hand.

And then, suddenly, silence.

Like a boat sailing out of a hurricane into a peaceful, sheltered lagoon, the Shadow Machine stopped shaking and grinding. The purple glow that had surrounded the twin orbs on the top was abruptly replaced by an array of new lights. Red, yellow, and blue, they chased each other all around the metal structure like fireflies.

And then there was a deep, sustained note like the tolling of an unimaginably huge bell. The sound resonated for miles around, shaking the ground with its rich, mellow tone.

As the note sounded, a ripple shot out from the heart of the machine. A disturbance in the air like a heat haze—a sphere of near-invisible energy expanding outward. And as it crossed Magpie, it wiped out his powers like an eraser. Mary, looking down on the scene, would never forget the sight of his purple energy disappearing as if it was wet paint being cleaned away. Nor would she ever forget what happened a split second later. The indescribable feeling that came over her as the energy passed across her own body. A feeling of warmth, of profound, ungraspable happiness, and of peace. And the unshakable conviction that her own Capability was suddenly back.

Below her, as the energy field passed across Murph, he was swept from the top of the Shadow Machine and fell hurtling toward the ground. Mary didn't hesitate. She sprang from the platform and dived into nothingness. Just like that day at Ribbon Robotics, she didn't stop to think. Umbrella-less, she plunged like a yellow shooting star, blurring in the air as she made straight for Murph. She gathered him up and floated gently back up to the platform, where Hilda's horses were waiting to greet them, cantering and neighing in delight.

"Oh good," said Murph groggily as the horses nuzzled at him. **"It worked."**

"Anything you'd like to share with the group, Cooper?" asked Mary airily. **"Like, ooh, I don't know, what the fish slicer has been going on for the past few weeks?** And today in particular? For one tiny, fleeting moment we thought you'd become best friends with *that* nasty piece of work." She pointed outward, to where the limp, unconscious

form of Magpie was now floating into view, carried by Angel, still flying.

Angel landed neatly on the balcony and dropped him onto the floor. Drained of his powers, Magpie looked incredibly old. His face seemed to have lost its expression of hate and malice. His eyes were sunken and his cheeks hollow.

"Angel, I can't lie, I'm a bit miffed that you just borrowed my Cape and you're already better at flying than I am," said Mary, smiling.

"You're just as good as me. I saw you flying without your umbrella. Maybe that's what an angel is?" said Angel casually. "Someone who shows you your own potential."

Hilda stamped her foot. "Well?" she asked Murph. "Are you going to ever actually explain what's going on? Like, ever? At all?"

"We reprogramed the Shadow Machine," explained Murph. "I mean, I knew the only way to try to help you guys was to play Magpie at his own game and take a power. But he got too confident. He thought I'd choose something obvious like invisibility or superstrength. But he slipped up. He told me that *all* his powers were in there. So I knew, if I looked hard enough, I'd find his original one. Magpie built that machine . . ."

"So, to beat it, you had to become Magpie . . ." breathed Hilda dramatically.

"Well, kind of, I guess," said Murph.

"And now it's releasing the stolen powers . . ." Mary went on.

"And giving them back," Murph confirmed. "Yeah. Clever, eh?"

"Don't get cocky," she warned him. "That was a pretty daring move, Cooper! We thought you'd gone totally power-crazy for a moment there."

"I know, sorry," said Murph bashfully. "There wasn't really time to explain. And it only just barely worked, thanks to Angel doubling up the tele-tech." He thought back to the sensation of Magpie's huge array of Capabilities coursing through his body and shivered slightly. "No wonder it started to overwhelm him in the end," he said softly. "It's a scary thing, that level of power." He shook himself, as if trying to clear the memory of a vivid nightmare.

"Quite fun, though," interjected Angel.

The rest of the Zeroes looked at her disapprovingly.

"For a bit!" she added, laughing nervously. "But, yeah, you know, ultimately, not good!"

"Hmmm. Speaking of Capes . . . I take it *you* don't have yours anymore, then, Murph?" Hilda wanted to know.

"I'm delighted to say you're absolutely right," answered Kid Normal.

And the ball of clear energy from the Shadow Machine continued to expand, zooming out around the planet, returning what had been stolen . . .

Carl and Flora had been watching the live broadcast from Titan Thirteen, crouched behind a burned-out, smoking popcorn stand. Flora was dressed in her Blue Phantom armor but had taken her helmet off so her husband could tend to a large cut on her forehead.

"We've got to get there and help them!" said Carl for the seventeenth time, as the footage on their HALO unit showed Magpie turning around and firing energy bolts.

"I know!" said Flora, also for the seventeenth time. "But what about Geoffrey over there? Frankly, I think he might have bitten off more than he can chew this time."

"What's the matter? Aren't you enjoying my little party?" screamed

the voice of Party Animal, sounding frighteningly close by. Carl poked his head out gingerly from behind the popcorn stand to see Mr. Geoffrey Souperman trussed up securely in a cocoon of brightly colored streamers. The monstrous clown was advancing on him through the ruins of a fairground.

"You won't get away this time, Party Animal," said Mr. Souperman dramatically. "It is I, Captain Alpha, your arch men . . . anemone . . . menesis."

"It's 'nemesis,'" sighed Flora. "When will he ever learn?"

"The rest of your little friends seem to be all partied out, Captain Alpha!" screeched the clown, gesturing toward the unconscious forms of the rest of their Heroes' Alliance unit, piled up at the entrance to a circus big top. "And now I have you at my mercy. **Prepare to**

party! No, not party. What's the word I want? Ah, yes, that's it. **DIE! Prepare to die, Captain!"**

"We won't stand a chance out there," whispered Carl. On cue, a balloon trumpeted past them and exploded not far away.

"We've got to try," said Flora decisively. "We can't leave Geoffrey. And if it does turn out to be our last stand . . . well, let's give them a show to remember. Ready?"

"Ready," agreed Carl, reaching out to take her hand.

"Ooooh, more little friends have come out to play!" yelled the clown as Flora and Carl stepped out from behind the ruined stand. "Come on then, you guys. **Let's PAAAAAAR- TAAAY!"** He filled his hands with balloons as they ran toward him, preparing to strike.

But as they ran, Flora felt a peculiar sensation, as if a ripple in the air had passed across them. She turned to Carl, an expression of pure wonder on her face. "I think we just gained a slight advantage, dear," she said softly. And she shimmered, and then vanished.

Carl stopped in surprise, and so did Party Animal. "Where did she go?" the clown asked sharply, going for the obvious question. "Didn't she want to party? Never mind, old man. We can still have a lot of fun together, can't we?"

"I don't think so, actually," said a voice from behind him. Party Animal spun frantically around, trying to identify where it was coming from. "You see," the voice continued, "you've got to know when to stop the party, my friend. Go on too long . . . and it always ends in tears."

The Blue Phantom materialized in midair in front of him, one foot already outstretched in a roundhouse kick. There was a hugely impressive noise, like a giant clown getting booted in the face, as her foot made contact. Party Animal keeled over like a popped parade balloon, as Flora made a perfect landing on his giant tummy and Carl danced from foot to foot in a jig of pure joy.

"Splendid work!" said Mr. Souperman warmly from his cocoon. "I knew we could take him."

Flora and Carl were oblivious to him as they hugged delightedly.

"Um . . . any chance someone could untie me at all?" asked Captain Alpha.

At Witchberry Hall, Sir Jasper Rowntree had watched Magpie's broadcast in dismay. The signal from Titan Thirteen had jammed the whole HALO network, so he was forced to watch impotently as Murph entered the Shadow Machine.

"Plucky young so-and-so," he mourned, shaking his head. "He had the makings of a real Hero. Shame it had to end like this."

When the battle began, the old man grew more and more confused. How on earth was young Cooper keeping Magpie at bay? What was going on? The footage from the cameras grew shaky, obscured by smoke and dust. He just barely caught sight of Magpie firing off bolts of electricity, and once he thought he saw Angel's silvery hair.

"What on earth . . . How did she get there . . . ?" he muttered to himself. "I told those kids to wait for backup. I suppose they didn't listen. I wouldn't have, either, to be fair."

But the most incredible thing of all happened shortly after that. There was a shift in the air, as if an invisible force field had rippled across the room.

"Great Scott of the Antarctic!" exclaimed Sir Jasper. **"I feel like I've had an upgrade!"** He gestured toward the HALO screen, and it immediately flickered and changed. SYSTEM READY, read the calm green letters. "I'm back in control!" marveled Tech Knight. "My Cape's come back! This is absolutely bananas!"

"Ber-ner-ner?" came a voice from outside the doorway.

"No, no, not now, thank you, Malcolm," said Sir Jasper absently. The giant monkey had turned out to be surprisingly gentle when fed regular supplies of what the staff at Witchberry Hall were now referring to as "yellow bendies." He seemed much happier staying in his monkey shape, in fact, and had even been helping out with some light Alliance duties.

"I'll fetch you a nice yellow bendy in a minute," the old man went on. "First I've got something to attend to."

He bent forward to the HALO unit and concentrated. The message changed, to read simply: TRANSMITTING.

"Attention, all units of the Heroes' Alliance," he said. **"This is Tech Knight. Kid Normal has defeated Magpie. Repeat, Kid Normal has defeated Magpie.** HALO system back online."

And the broadcasts came back from the units of the Alliance. Cheers, whoops, and squeals of victory rang out from the speakers as Sir Jasper Rowntree clapped his hands together in pure joy.

"Just leave me here under the tree, Butler, and bring me a grilled cheese and a refreshing glass of Kool-Aid, there's a good chap." Wayne Blaze, sitting in a wheelchair with a tartan blanket draped across his knees, sighed as he looked out across the immaculately landscaped gardens of Blaze Mansion. His butler, Butler, shuffled off across the lawn to fetch his bedtime snack.

Once, long ago, Blaze had been a crime-fighting Hero of the Golden Age known as the Dandy Man. Dressed as a highwayman (for reasons that nobody under forty will ever fully understand) he had used his Capability to transform his hands into swords, to battle evil wherever he found it. Until he had become Magpie's first victim one fateful night at Nakamura Tower.

Blaze watched the bats swooping above the grounds, black flashes against the evening sky. He sang to himself—a soft, melancholy song—as he remembered his glory days of long ago.

"Her name is Rio, and she dances on the sand . . ."

The bats above the garden wheeled in a different pattern as their sensitive sonar detected a disturbance in the air. Wayne Blaze shivered as a slight breeze seemed to pass across him—then he sat up sharply. **"Butler!"** he cried.

"Yes, sir?" replied Butler, who was approaching with a silver tray bearing a grilled cheese and a glass of juice.

"I just had the most peculiar sensation!" exclaimed Blaze.

"I shall fetch your spare pants, sir," said Butler wearily.

"No, no, not that," snapped Blaze, looking embarrassed. "I think . . . Do you know, I really do think . . . the Dandy Man is back!"

Butler began to respond, but was silenced as his employer suddenly got out of his wheelchair, tossing the tartan blanket high into the air. Two bright swords flashed in the twilight, cutting the blanket to ribbons. It floated back to earth like confetti at a very Scottish wedding, as the Dandy Man turned delightedly to his trusty companion.

"Da diddly, qua-qua!" he shouted in glee. "Butler, fetch my highwayman's hat! **I'm back, baby!"**

Back at Titan Thirteen, the gears and wheels of the Shadow Machine slowed to a halt. The last stolen Cape had been returned. Its job was done.

"Okay, right," said Murph matter-of-factly, **"that gives us about ten minutes to get out of here before this whole place explodes."**

"That," said Billy with a pained expression, "is in very real danger of becoming your catchphrase. I mean, seriously? *More* exploding buildings?"

"There was no way I was going to leave that machine intact," said Murph decisively. "It's too dangerous in the wrong hands, so while we were up there, I reprogrammed it so that returning the powers would be its final task and—" He broke off as a sudden shout came from behind him.

"Murph!" Nellie was standing by the electronic keypad to the cell door, with her familiar blue lightning energy once again dancing in her hand. The keypad was sparking and flashing, the cell door was open, and his mom was pelting across the floor toward him, followed by Andy. The Super Zeroes cleared a path as she rushed up to him like a guided missile—only the good kind—and swept him into her arms.

"Hey, Mom," said Murph weakly.

"So," she said after a few more seconds of really grade-A hugging, "you've all got superpowers, then?" The others shuffled their feet sheepishly. "Didn't anybody think this was worth mentioning at all?"

"You would have taken me out of The School in a heartbeat, Mom!" protested Murph. "And it's the only place . . ."

"The only place you've made real friends in years," his mom finished for him, her face softening.

"Anyway . . . shall we continue this conversation

when we've escaped the building before it explodes?" asked Billy sensibly.

This seemed to everyone to be an excellent idea.

"Somebody help me pick him up," said Murph, grabbing Magpie's arms. "He's not going to cause any problems. His is the one power I didn't let the Shadow Machine return. We'll take him back to Witchberry Hall."

The old man was featherlight, his arms and legs flopping as they carried him down the stairs, along the brick passageway, and into the *Banshee*. Murph's mom joined the Super Zeroes in the car. Andy seemed eager to go with Angel, who had salvaged the *Wyvern* and was already astride it, ready for takeoff.

"I am so going on the flying motorcycle!" Andy enthused. "Just call me Dumbledore."

"Who's Bumble Door?" Angel wanted to know, but her education in twenty-first-century culture would have to wait for another day.

There was a scream from the *Banshee*'s jet engines as Nellie folded up the ramp and turned to her friends. "Mom and brother rescued," she checked off. "Magpie defeated. Stolen Capes returned. Not a bad night's work, Cooper."

Murph smiled tentatively.

"Escape building prior to huge explosion?" suggested Billy nervously.

The pilot nodded, firing up the twin jets as Angel steered the *Wyvern* into the sky. Together they banked over the concrete chimneys of Titan Thirteen and soared away into the night.

They were already miles away when the Shadow Machine exploded.

19

The Overview Effect

The bright white fireball that engulfed Titan Thirteen as the Shadow Machine exploded was visible from space. (Actually, more or less everything is visible from space; it just depends how big your telescope is. You could be visible from space yourself, especially if you jumped around a bit, waving and going, "Hey, astronauts, look at me!" Give it a try.)

But what we mean is, the Titan Thirteen explosion was visible from space, even without using a telescope. Here's an example.

Professor Brian Moon, world famous cosmologist, was sitting in the International Space Station, where he was spending a couple of weeks to get away from it all and be alone with his elementary particles. He was just gazing out of the window, watching a beautiful moonset (which is a real word and a very good one) and pondering the mysteries of the universe, as per usual.

When you think about it, thought Professor Brian Moon to himself, *the world is just like an orange, only covered in blue and green mold. And the moon is a bit like an egg. And perhaps that's all we are, really, when you think about it. Just little people scuttling around on a moldy old orange with a giant egg in geostationary orbit around it. Only an egg made of cheese. Ooh, cheese.*

He really missed cheese. You can't get proper cheese in space. It's all freeze-dried and very difficult to put on a cracker. Not that it matters, because you can't really get crackers either. And you have to go to the bathroom inside your space suit sometimes. It's overrated, space.

Anyway, as chance would have it (it's not really chance: we made it up this way—but let's not get all metaphysical about it. There isn't time. This was only supposed to be a quick aside and it's already spreading over two pages). Anyway, as chance would have it, he was passing over the continent of Europe at that very moment. *Ooh, Europe*, thought the professor, *they have lovely cheese down there, don't they? I love cheese, me. And perhaps that's all I am, you know, when you really think about it. Just a professor who really likes cheese . . . hang on. What on earth is that?*

A piercingly bright flash erupted from the dark planet below him, a white circular shock wave that radiated out from a single point and only dispersed after several seconds.

Holy smoke, thought Professor Brian Moon to himself. *Whatever that explosion was, it was big enough to be visible all the way up here, in actual space.* (Told you.)

As well as being visible from space, the explosion was also extremely noticeable back on earth. Hundreds of miles away, people saw a flash of white in the distant night sky and thought to themselves, *There's a storm coming.*

*

The *Banshee* shook in a patch of sudden turbulence as the shock wave from the exploding Shadow Machine overtook them.

"There it goes," said Murph, looking out of the back window of the *Banshee* at the fireball expanding up into the night sky.

"The Cleaners will have a hard job explaining that one away," mused Hilda.

"Yeah, you know that whole 'The world of Heroes operates in total secrecy' thing?" said Billy. "I think that might just have gone up in smoke."

"Well, we're certainly getting a lot of well-wishers radioing in to send their congratulations and relief. Look at this thing!" Mary pointed to one of the display screens in the cockpit next to Nellie. "I've never seen so many messages!"

"I just can't quite believe my little Murph is part of all this!" said Murph's mom shakily from the floor. "I was always worried you'd begin keeping secrets from me when you started growing up, but I was more thinking about you having a party when I was away for the night. This"—she gestured around at the interior of the flying car—"this is next-level, I've got to admit."

"Yeah, about that . . ." began Murph. Then he stopped and wondered where on earth to begin unraveling this for her.

"He's a Hero," came Mary's voice. She was strapped into the copilot's seat. "He saved the whole school last year. And he fought against the most powerful villain there is. He rescued our friend's daughter when everyone thought she'd been dead for thirty years. And . . ."

"And he rescued me," Murph's mom finished for her. "You all did. You flew all the way in your . . . your . . ."

"It's called the *Banshee*, Ms. Cooper," piped up Nellie shyly.

"And on a flying motorcycle . . ." added Murph's mom as if she could barely believe what she was saying.

"You always said you wanted to find me a school with great extracurricular activities," deadpanned Murph as the *Banshee* roared on into the night.

As dawn broke, the Super Zeroes sat on Murph's balcony watching the new day prepare to do its thing. The first rays of the rising sun were just snaking over the horizon, daubing the clouds with patches of watercolor pink. A single bird trilled a high, constant liquid song as it hovered far overhead.

Hours before, there had been embarrassing cheering at Witchberry Hall when they had delivered Magpie to the Heroes' Alliance. Flora and Carl were still out, helping to mop up the Alliance of Evil, but a beaming Miss Flint had been fulsome in her praise.

"The whole Alliance saw your selflessness," she had congratulated Murph. "And your bravery . . . well, it won't go unrewarded. And I owe you an apology too, it seems, Mr. Cooper. Magpie was more devious than even I could have predicted. I never suspected he was blackmailing one of our top operatives. I hope you can forgive me for my harsh words. All of you."

But all the five friends had really wanted to do was spend some time together. Pleading tiredness, they had left the rest of the congratulations for another time and flown back to Murph's house.

"That," said Billy meditatively as the sun showed a glistening sliver above the far horizon, "was a bad one."

"Nah," said Murph casually. "Could have been worse." He coughed an embarrassed cough. "Seriously though," he told his friends, "I can't believe you followed me. You wouldn't have if you'd known it was me that got us kicked out of the Alliance."

"But we did know!" answered Mary. **"I heard you talking to Magpie in the garden!"**

"What?" Murph was dumbfounded. "You knew! You knew I'd been helping him . . ."

"And we came anyway," Mary finished for him.

"But you said—"

She cut him off quickly, blushing. "We all said things we didn't mean. It was all part of Magpie's awful mind games. I see that now."

They paused as the birdsong bubbled above them, taking in what had happened.

"We actually faced Magpie!" said Hilda, awestruck. "On our own. And he stole our powers!"

"No he didn't," answered Kid Normal.

"Wha . . . *what*?" faltered Mary.

"He didn't steal your powers," repeated Murph. "He didn't steal your bravery, Mary, or your cool, or your . . . sass, or your intelligence. And Nellie, he didn't steal your skills as an engineer, or as a pilot, or your . . . your loyalty to your friends."

Nellie, her cheeks flushed, stood up and braced her legs. She seemed shaken but deeply moved by what Murph was saying.

"Billy . . ." he continued, suddenly feeling like he was addressing a whole school assembly without a script, and understanding for the first time why Mr. Souperman got so flustered when he gave speeches. "He didn't steal your sense of humor, or your ability to get us out of a tight spot time and time again."

"Do me, do me!" pleaded Hilda.

"Hilda . . . He didn't steal your love for the world of Heroes, or your determination. Or your kick-butt drawing ability. Or your bassoon-playing skills!"

"Or your truly awesome hair!" added Billy, making Hilda blush. **"And, Mary, he didn't take your cool fashion sense,"** he went on, warming to the theme. Murph was heartily glad that someone else had joined in. But Billy wasn't the only one.

Hilda had gotten to her feet. "Billy," she said—her voice shaky but determined—"remember when Mr. Flash had been mind-controlled, and you kept him talking so we could escape? Magpie can't take that away. And, Mary, he could never steal the way you're calm and collected when everything seems hopeless. Nellie . . . You just love to be you, and you don't care what anyone thinks. You don't feel you have to fill up spaces with a lot of chat. And I really, *really* like your sweater." Tears were running down her face, but she was smiling.

Murph looked at Angel, who was sitting quietly, a little apart from the five friends.

"Angel", said Murph, "thank you for everything today. Your skill on the *Wyvern* . . . your quick thinking on top of the Shadow Machine. I couldn't have done it without you. You're a force to be reckoned with."

"We're lucky to have you on the team," added Mary, smiling.

Angel had turned the color of a perfectly ripe tomato. "It was a privilege to fight alongside you," she said.

"Thanks for letting me take on Magpie . . . not just for myself, but for my mom and dad, too. They lost me for thirty years because of him. So . . . thanks for letting me tag along." She reached out a hand. "Especially you, Mary. Thanks."

They had an awkward high-five/hand-holding moment.

"And," added Angel joyfully, "I'm so pleased you all got your Capes back—'cause now I can borrow them!"

"Hmm. Except little old me," said Murph melodramatically. "I didn't have a power for him to steal in the first place."

"Wrong!" said Mary. The others were shaking their heads too.

"You have powers that Magpie's desperate to steal," Nellie told him, coming forward and laying a hand on his shoulder. "That's why he can't stand you. Look at what he did just to try to get inside your head."

"Remember that day we went up against Nektar?" Mary piped up. "I said it that day too. You're the bravest person I know. You see things other people can't see."

"Well, now I understand what it's like to have a power to lose, at least," mused Murph.

"That makes you really quite unique, you know," said Mary seriously, reaching out to take his hand and looking at him intently. "How do you feel?"

"Honestly?" said Murph. "Relieved. Completely and utterly relieved that, with this all over, I don't have to let you down anymore. Relieved that I don't have to lie anymore. Relieved that I have my friends back, and relieved that they didn't desert me."

"We'd never have deserted you,"

replied Mary. "But seriously . . . what was it like to have all those Capes?"

Murph thought about his answer. "It's hard to explain," he told her slowly. "I'm still taking it in, I think. It was . . . overwhelming. It would have driven me crazy, for sure, if I'd kept them. Like Magpie. But it's helped me understand . . . what power can do. Does that make sense? How the people who really want it are usually the ones who shouldn't have it."

"It's like the Overview Effect," said Mary. "That's what astronauts have, once they've seen the earth from space. They talk about having a larger perspective—about seeing the bigger picture. For a few moments there, you were one of the most powerful Heroes who ever existed."

"And now I'm back to being Kid Normal," said Murph gratefully.

Mary smiled at him, withdrew her hand, and clapped him on the shoulder. "Kid Normal's not such a bad Hero, you know," she told him.

"With his team around him," Murph clarified. **"What's a Hero without his Zeroes?"**

"What's anyone without their friends?" agreed Mary.

They were silent for a long moment, not because they had nothing to say to each other, but because there was plenty of time to say it.

THE END . . .

20

The Bit After the End

The air around the Titan Thirteen power plant was still thick with choking dust, the flashing lights of the emergency vehicles casting unearthly blue rainbows through the murk. A cordon of plastic tape had been strung around the entire site, bearing the words TOXIC HAZARD—DO NOT ENTER. And behind this was ranged a milling crowd of bystanders, TV crews, police officers and men and women in black military-style uniforms.

Inside the tape, ghostly silhouettes could be seen as rescue crews crunched across the rubble in their heavy boots, some holding leashes on which large sniffer dogs strained and whined in frustration.

At the edge of the ruins lay the collapsed concrete towers, broken into huge lumps like the discarded building blocks of some stone giant. Beyond this, there was barely a wall standing. Bricks, metal pipes, and girders were littered around, seemingly at random.

Suddenly there was a frantic barking. One of the dogs had homed in on an area that may once have been a large open space in the center of the power plant. It was digging with its paws at one corner, where a triangle of beaten, scarred metal was visible.

"There's something here!"

The rescue crews converged.

"Careful!"
"It's a door!"

Gradually, painstakingly, the rubble was cleared. Gloved hands flung bricks to one side to reveal a metal chamber. Despite being heavily reinforced and riveted, it was badly damaged. And, as it was forced open, a small chamber was revealed, almost completely buried underneath the debris.

The sniffer dog whined in confusion, then fell silent.

As the rescuers watched, a man climbed out of the

door, brushing down his dark suit with long fingers and smoothing his hair with the other hand. A sudden jet of light from a flashlight cut through the gloom, reflecting off his highly polished shoes.

"We've found someone!" one of the emergency crews yelled. **"Stand by!"**

The news crews behind the plastic tape stirred and buzzed excitedly like a swarm of wasps, raising their cameras and microphones to capture the miraculous moment. Powerful lights were ignited, beaming through the dust to reveal a man walking through the rubble toward them, brushing off the supporting hands that were being offered to him by rescuers on either side.

"I have something to say," said Nicholas Knox in a commanding, strident voice as the eyes of the media focused on his keen, sharp-nosed face. **"The country deserves to know what happened here today. We have been lied to for too long. I have uncovered a shocking secret."**

It's not difficult to control people's minds, he thought to himself as the cameras started to roll.

You just have to give them something to be afraid of.

THANKS...

First of all, thanks to **YOU** for reading our story.

Now go and write your own!

Thanks to our agent, **Stephanie Thwaites**,

for brilliance and brunch, and our editor,

Hannah Sandford, for patience and pastries.

You are both the best in the business.

Thanks, **Erica**, for bringing the world of Kid Normal

to life—you are incredible.

Au revoir and bon voyage to **Andrea Kearney**,

Emma Bradshaw, and **Charlotte Armstrong**—

Team Normal for life!

Thanks to everyone at Bloomsbury for literally

being the best, including (but not limited to) **Nigel,**

Emma, Rebecca, Ian, Bea, Jade, Sarah,

Fliss, Cal, Glen, Kate, all the Emilys, and the incredible **rights team,** who help Murph and his friends fly around the world.

Massive thanks to everyone who comes to see us at festivals, school visits, and book signings. We love chatting to each and every one of you.

And thanks to the Masons Arms and Nando's, where we plot, scheme, write, and eat chicken, not necessarily in that order.

CHRIS WOULD ALSO LIKE TO SAY: Massive thanks to Lucas, who is awesome, but not to Mabel, because she was no help at all and just wanted to lie down on the laptop all the time. I'm truly grateful to all the authors who have been so kind and welcoming, especially Anna James and Maz Evans. And thanks to Shed Seven, anyone who helps run a library or uses a library, and every single person involved in the manufacture and retailing of cheese.

AND FROM GREG: As well as all those Chris thanked, an extra nod to my family, who keep me going at all times; to the listeners of *Radio 1*, who keep me on my toes at all times; to my friends, who keep me on the ground at all times; and, most importantly, to my wonderful pal Chris, who keeps me laughing at all times. A funnier and more talented man you will not find. I couldn't be more proud of the world we've created. Kid Normal literally (and literarily) wouldn't exist without your wonderful mind. On to the next one! (After some wine and a holiday.)